NORTH BRISTOL WRITERS

IN ASSOCIATION WITH IANDE PRESS

TALES *from the* GRAVEYARD

Edited by
Eric Nash & Peter Sutton

NORTH BRISTOL WRITERS

First published in 2018
by North Bristol Writers
in association with Iande Press
www.northbristolwriters.wordpress.com

Edited by Eric Nash & Peter Sutton.

Three Billion Heartbeats, Give or Take © Kevlin Henney
Needle and Thread © Clare Dornan | *Gravewatcher* © Chrissey Harrison
Work Experience © Jon Charles | *Angel* © Louise Gethin
Once The Trees © Grace Palmer | *Darkfall* © Dev Agarwal
Unwelcome © Amanda Staples | *Unforgotten* © Ken Shinn
Graveyard Shift © Jay Millington | *All The Moor Remembers* © Chloe Headdon
What Dwells In The Mind © Scott Lewis | *Abra-Cadaver* © Maria Herring
The Silent Scream © Tanwen Cooper | *Messenger* © Alex Ballinger
Blood Thicker Than Water © Piotr Świetlik

Cover artwork © Fabrice Mazat
Cover design and typeset by Chrissey Harrison
Photographs, illustrations & other attributions - see pg263

A CIP catalogue record of this book is available
from the British Library

ISBN 978-0-9554182-4-2
ebook available - ISBN 978-0-9554182-5-9

Printed and bound in the UK by IngramSpark

Contents

Introduction

And we come to the third book from North Bristol Writers. Way back in 2013 when I first started trying to get some short stories published I came across the North Bristol Creative Writing Group (now we are just North Bristol Writers) on Facebook and, living in north Bristol, asked to join. It turned out that the group was pretty much moribund at the time but Jemma (the organiser of the group) agreed to start up bimonthly meetings again if I could attract a few more writers. So I did and we met and we talked about writing and we critiqued and we workshopped and in 2015 we produced an anthology—*North by Southwest*—via a crowdfunding campaign. In 2016 we brought out our second—*The Dark Half of the Year*—which I edited with Ian Millsted. And here in your hand is the third.

Some of the same writers recur of course, some have been there from near the start. It is interesting to note the changes and the writers we have drawn in from beyond in each book. It's been a pleasure to edit these fine writers and I feel that this completes a 'dark tales' duology, with a fourth book set to venture into new territory.

So why graveyards? Our last book, and this one, were spawned from events. The North Bristol Writers have performed at the Bristol Festival of Literature each year for several years. Both *The Dark Half of the Year* and this book first saw dark of night as collections of performance pieces read at Arnos Vale cemetery, a place that recurs many times throughout the various stories within.

Within, some of those original pieces are substantially altered, some are missing and new ones are added. Bristol Festival of Literature occurs in October every year and near Halloween so it's been fun to play with dark themes and ghost tales.

We start with Kevlin Henney again, he also started *The Dark Half of the Year*, and finished *North by Southwest.* Kevlin writes very short tales, tightly packed with character and emotion, and this one packs a punch. His tale here sets us up nicely for a mix of dark tales—some personal, some apocalyptic, some startling.

Of course there are ghostly and ghoulish tales—like ghostly *Work Experience* by Jon Charles and ghoulish *Abra-Cadaver* by Maria Herring. But there are also some innovative twist on the subject of graveyards like Unforgotten by Ken Shinn and Graveyard Shift by Jay Millington.

Scott Lewis's *What Dwells in the Mind* reminds the reader of classic Weird Tales whilst *Messenger* by Alex Ballinger is bang up to date, seamlessly weaving in the modern into an entertainingly dark tale.

What I'm trying to say is that there is a wide selection although the theme seems like it would produce a narrow collection of tales.

It's very tempting to extol the virtues of every single story in the book—I've not yet mentioned Chrissey Harrison's longer but full of heart *Gravewatcher* or, or... but perhaps you should dive in and become as enamoured of them by reading as I have become by editing them.

It's also traditional to thank people—in the absence of an acknowledgements section I'd like to thank Eric for choosing the stories and putting them in the right order, Ian for valuable opinions on the choices, Chrissey for typesetting and cover text and photographs and proofreading and everything else (seriously doubt if anyone has put in more work on this book than her), Fab for the cover illustration (which is brilliant), all the writers that submitted (consolations for the ones that didn't make it) and all the writers who critiqued the stories (that made the editing easier!)

And you, dear reader, thanks for reading—I know you'll enjoy it. If you do please tell your friends, leave us a review on Amazon and buy our other books!

Peter Sutton
EDITOR

Three Billion Heartbeats, Give or Take

Kevlin Henney

A billion heartbeats, give or take. That's all you've got.

So they say.

Doesn't matter if you're a man or a mouse, a lion or a dog, life is rationed. You live your lot. You use your quota.

Unless it's taken from you.

A billion heartbeats. I'm counting every one. They're coming thick and fast, each pulse feeding the wet earth with the blood from my leg. Maggie's lying on top of me at the bottom of this hole, my blood running and pooling with hers. No more than a hint of moonlight. Not enough to see her eyes, but they'll still be holding the same fear they held when I pulled her into this hole. Fear, regret, sorrow... rain, like tears, running off her face onto mine.

Breathe slow. Breathe quiet. Hold in the pain and lie still. Lie like I belong at the bottom of this hole. Lie like prey.

"Tom Mitchell, where are you?" Predator. "I know you're here. I know you're hit. I heard you cry out." Her voice is getting closer.

Maggie said she thought she was being followed. Maggie said a lot of things. Maggie did a lot of things. She didn't always make sense, but I always tried to help. Mostly it was people help—landlords, dealers, pimps— but sometimes it was money help. Not that I had much, but of the two straws we drew twenty-some years ago she got the shorter one. When we fell apart she fell further. But I still looked out for her—more big brother than ex-lover.

Enough a part of her life I'd made the roll call on her arm. *Mum, Dad, Eric, Sam, Tom...* least, I'm guessing that's me. Never asked. Never asked about the others. Tried not to look. The names appeared one year, home-inked tattoos scratched into her arm, sharing skin with needle marks and razor scars. Never noticed any new names since.

Till this afternoon I hadn't heard from her in years— three years, the day of her uncle's funeral. Then she'd been upset, crying. I didn't say anything; she just needed a voice at the other end of the phone. Today... today was different.

"Tom, I'm being followed. I'm scared."

"Who is he?"

"It's a woman. I don't know who she is, but I see her wherever I go. Asda, post office, pub. Everywhere."

"Calm down, Maggie. She's probably just one of those faces you see on the high street. You're always going to run into people who live around you."

"Tom, you're not listening! She's everywhere. Not

just round here, not even just London, everywhere. I went to see my dad in Southend: she was there. She got off the same bus."

I said I'd meet her tonight. Calm her down, find out what she'd got herself into—or onto. See if her mind was playing tricks on her. See if her imagination had got outside help.

It hadn't. The text I got after her call made it real: *glad she got in touch w u. want 2 c u 2.* Unknown number. No response when I called back.

Maggie wasn't where we'd agreed to meet, a couple of roads down from the cemetery, outside The Griffin. Being late wasn't unusual, but another text from the same unknown number—it just said *cemetery*—had me running, all my thoughts on hold.

Haven't been back in years. There's work enough if you're ex-army, but not many jobs for those who then pass through Her Majesty's Prison Service. Gravedigger is not one you get sentimental about. No matter what happens in life, fate puts you in a hole. I was just someone that dug the holes, ready and waiting.

And here I am, at the bottom of one that was ready. Waiting.

This cemetery's not exactly one of London's finest, not one for the tourists—no mausoleums, no ornate headstones, nobody famous. Most well-known person buried here is Marj Walker. She owned a sewing shop opposite The Griffin, did all the good causes, did all the right things, everyone who knew her loved her. Apparently. There's no fancy headstones round here, but Marj's daughter put her old sewing machines on the grave. Nice touch. Sentimental. Rusted solid in no time.

"Shit. Where are you?" From above, to herself. The woman's looking down, looking in, wild-haired silhouette against the rain and light pollution, looking at Maggie's back and the mud-lined tomb. "Where are you, Tom Mitchell?" Louder, to the rain, the stones and anyone else in earshot.

Lying still, I gaze into Maggie's eyes. Fear looks back. But nothing more.

First and last time in three years. I ran, but... I found her lying next to an open grave, staring up into the rain, already gone. A shot through her leg, another through her heart. First to wing her, second to finish her.

I held her close, whispering all the things I should've said years ago.

Gunshot broke the mourning, knocking me back, but the bullet had hit Maggie. Looking up, I saw a young woman coming out of the trees. Too far and too dark to read her face, but the glint of a handgun made her meaning clear enough. I started to shuffle back, looking for cover, still holding onto Maggie, holding her for protection, roles reversed after all these years.

The woman brought her arms together, raising them.

A shot. Missed.

Another. Through my thigh. Jesus. Fuck.

All those years in the army, the nick and the streets and never took a bullet. Never too late to start, but I couldn't think for the pain. I needed cover. Fast.

I rolled into the open grave, bringing Maggie over with me, hoping distance, darkness and rain had hidden my move.

It had.

"You can't hide!" She's moving away. "Don't know if we're going to get the chance to have a little chat like I did with Mum." Mum? "So where are you, Dad? Didn't know you had a daughter? Didn't Mum tell you?"

She needs to keep talking, but I need to stop listening. Need to think straight—whatever she's saying, whatever my leg's screaming. Ignore the pain, ignore the words, hear the voice—the voice I now realise sounds so like Maggie's... no, need to hear where it is, not what it is. Hear where she is. Think.

I roll Maggie off me and pull myself up on my other leg. I put my head over the edge and see the woman—daughter?—a few headstones away, her back to me, looking round. I pull myself out the hole—*six-foot under's* a saying not a spec. Need to think predator, not prey. Use the night. Use the rain. Use the cemetery. Concentrate, breathe, move. Think, but not about the pain—save that for later.

"Didn't you wonder why she was so messed up when you came back? More messed up than usual, more messed up than when you ran off to play soldiers? Bit of a case already, wasn't she?" She's pacing, looking round, her voice loud at first then lost to rain as she turns, then back again. "Mum ever tell you about Uncle Eric? Don't think she did. Kept him and what he did to her from you as well. All a secret. Like he told her to keep it. She told me all kinds of stuff. Uncle Eric. Three years gone. But not forgotten. Shame I didn't get to him first."

I know where I am. It's not far. Two plots. I'm rolling,

shuffling, covered in mud, covered in camouflage, but I need her to come closer.

"Mum could've loved me. Should've loved me. Should've cared. If you'd been there, it would've been different. If you'd cared. Even after, if you'd cared, you'd have noticed, worked it out, found out about me, found me." Coming closer. "She gave me up, your baby, your Samantha. Just another thing to be thrown away. Just another thing to be forgotten, like a rusted needle or a fucking john.

"But you and me are proper family. Like father, like daughter. Army loves a broken-home story. They don't like it when you take things, though. Eventually they'll notice when things—guns and petty cash—go missing. But it's all in a good cause." A click. Checking the magazine? "I'm not going to be forgotten. I want to be the rest of your life. I want you to share that with Mum."

I'm there, leaning against the headstone, out of sight. She's close enough. I move to a crouch, pushing the pain into silence.

I pull out my phone, kick off the ringtone and throw it onto the next plot.

She runs over. She picks it up—"Shit!"—looking up in time to see a rusted sewing machine coming at her.

One swing is all I can manage.

That's all it takes.

I fall to the ground with her. She's out, head bloody. Her blood, Maggie's and mine against the mud. Under cover of moonlight, beneath rain-washed blood and matted hair, I see what might be cheekbones like mine, what might be lips like Maggie's. What might be. What might have been.

I'm listening to my heart beating against the rain. A billion heartbeats, give or take. That's all you've got.

So they say.

You live your lot. You use your quota.

Unless it's taken from you. Sometimes at the end, sometimes at the start.

KEVLIN HENNEY

Kevlin Henney writes shorts and flashes and drabbles of fiction and books and articles on software development. His fiction has appeared online and on tree (*Daily Science Fiction, Litro, New Scientist, Physics World, Reflex Fiction, LabLit, Flight Journal* and many more) and has been included in a number of anthologies (*The Dark Half of the Year, North by Southwest, We Can Improve You, Haunted, Salt Anthology of New Writing, Ripening, Sleep Is a Beautiful Colour* and many more).

As well as having his work rejected and make no impression whatsoever on writing competitions, Kevlin's stories have been longlisted, shortlisted and placed, and he won the CrimeFest 2014 Flashbang contest. He reads at spoken word events, winning the National Flash-Fiction Day Oxford flash slam in 2012, and has performed his work on local radio (BBC Radio Bristol and Ujima). Kevlin has been involved in the organisation of the Bristol Festival of Literature and events for National Flash-Fiction Day.

He lives in Bristol and online, where he can stalked as @KevlinHenney on Twitter, @kevlinhenney on Medium and @kevlin.henney on Instagram.

Needle and Thread

CLARE DORNAN

Just inside the entrance to the graveyard, I can stand unnoticed with a clear view of the car park where she should arrive. I'm not the only one who is waiting for her; a small group has gathered, but she is late and they have started to wander through the graves that line the path.

I begin to mimic their movements: A step, a pause and a small lean forward to read the gravestone inscription. This slow and steady pacing is helping to contain my excitement but I still have to grip my hands tight. The twitching in my fingers becomes unbearable when they get impatient.

Finally, Helena Grigson's red Mini swerves through the cemetery gates and comes to an abrupt stop. Her dark hair is hanging loose around her shoulders—just as it is in the photograph on the back-cover of her book. She is all smiles and hands waving as she steps out of the car and the scattered group turn and move towards her, like iron filings drawn to a magnet.

I know how I appear to her. I'm a stooped old man

in a wool coat that's too long in the arms. Just another faceless fan of her book, queuing on a grey Sunday morning to hear her speak. My hands shake as I pass her my ticket and she takes it with a cursory smile before moving on.

But if she'd taken the time to look at me, to *really* look, maybe she wouldn't have dismissed me so easily. I have always suspected that my hands reveal who I really am. The clues are there in my fingers—so long and delicate. They can only belong to a craftsman who is highly skilled in precision. These hands of mine have perfected the art of gently teasing death up to the surface, until it is so close, I can smell it on their skin. Then death is mine to toy with, until I am ready to let it take them.

Helena Grigson leads the group up the steep tarmac path through the cemetery and onto a small, well-trodden grassy track. When she comes to a halt, she turns and her voice barks instructions for us to gather close. I join the circle forming around her and look down at the small gravestone at her feet. For the first time, after more than fifty years, I see where my family's remains are buried.

On a rough, mottled slab are three faintly carved names.

My mother's.

My father's.

And mine.

* * *

Helena clears her throat, claps her hands together and announces that we have arrived at the grave of the young man who was the inspiration for her novel: the murderer the police nick-named the Needle Man as he used to sew his victims' mouths shut, while they were still alive, using their own skin and hair.

I'm watching her speak, her eyes wide, theatrical. She flicks her hair, left, right, left, and I know what I will do with it later. I will pluck those long dark threads and they will glide easily through her lips. Then I will begin on her eyelids, her nostrils, her ears. I will embroider them slowly, until her words are sealed tight inside her head.

She opens her novel and begins to perform for her audience. I can see she enjoys enthralling these people with her bastardised version of my life. They are listening intently. A camera clicks behind me as some besotted fan captures her in action. She reads her crass description of my first victim's death before she flicks through to a page marker, looks up to ensure everyone is watching and regales us with her version of the thoughts running through my teenage mind.

Now she pauses and lowers her book. She says that it was purely by chance that she came across my diaries in the police records. And it was through these writings of mine that she gained an incredible insight into my 'uniquely tortured soul.' She tells us how moving it was to read of the terrible guilt I felt for the people I'd murdered and the agonising battles that raged within me when I tried to stop myself from killing.

It was, according to her, this internal conflict that led me on Christmas Day 1963 to write my suicide note and set myself alight in the family home. When my body, and those of my parents were retrieved from the ashes, they were burnt beyond recognition.

It's clear she does not suspect that my diaries are a work of fiction. I remember how amusing they were to write—though, I did wonder if I was overplaying the internal angst angle. Yet, they have fooled everyone who reads them. Even the esteemed Ms Helena Grigson.

What irks me though is not her naivety, or her greed for notoriety on the back of my achievements; it is her lack of appreciation for my artistry. She describes me as a butcher, not the craftsman that I am. Tonight, as I'll sew my way very slowly across her face, she will at least get to experience, first-hand, the great care I take with my work.

And, while I am with her, I will have plenty of time to educate her on the many details of my life that she has misunderstood. Though I will wait, until I am sure that death is just a sniff away, before I explain that it was my brother who was locked in my room and set alight to die with my parents. And how, once my family were out of the way, it was surprisingly easy to take my brother's identity and slip away.

I might even confess my one lasting regret over the

death of my family. I didn't sew my family into silence before they died. At night their voices still chatter in my head.

She closes her book, soaks up the smattering of applause and signals for the group to set off down the hill. I stay back and let them go ahead. I need a moment alone to savour what will soon begin. Yet a middle-aged woman also stays behind waiting for the others to leave.

She is crouching by my gravestone taking photos. She frowns at the camera screen before she looks up and notices me.

"It's not as impressive as I thought it would be," she says with an American accent.

"And I think they've spelt his name wrong." She scratches the moss off my name and as I step closer I can see that she's right.

"Yes. It should have two t's" I say, "Elliott with two t's. The council must have done it on the cheap."

She looks up and laughs loudly. "Are you another fan of the Needle Man?"

I smile back at her. "Do murderers have fans?"

"This one does, for sure," she says holding her hand out towards me. "I'm Molly Sturlen, I'm researching a screenplay about this guy. I've gotta say, he was quite a character."

So, yet another person trying to profit from my art. Another parasite with no imagination of their own. I shake her hand and feel the softness of her skin. Her hair is blonde, dyed and barely an inch long. It's too short to be useful. Yet her hands are moisturised and pampered: her skin would peel easily.

I turn quickly and walk away; I have no time for these distractions. Helena will already be close to the car park. She will answer questions from her adoring fans and maybe sign a few copies of her ridiculous book, but I must reach the car park before she leaves.

Yet this American has begun to walk alongside me.

"I've got to say I'm curious," she says, "How did you know about his name? I didn't think it was common knowledge?"

I ignore her and walk on, but I can feel she is looking at me closely. I glance across and see a small vein throbbing on the side of her eye. Sometimes I make a neat parallel cut near the eyelid and hook those veins out with a needle. I carry on walking but I can't resist.

"I grew up around here," I say.

Her eyes light up, and the little vein pulses harder. Veins can be surprisingly long if you tease them out slowly. Then they slice nicely into small, sinuous threads.

"Did you know him?" She is eager, excited and I give a small nod. She lays a hand on my arm to slow me down.

"Could you tell me what he was like? Was he a really strange kid?"

I shrug and try to move on, but she steps ahead and blocks my path.

"Look," she says, "I'm only here for the next two days, then I am back to the US. I would love to hear anything about him. Can I give you a lift somewhere we could get coffee?"

I can see past her shoulder to the car park below. Helena Grigson is already walking towards her red Mini. No one is talking to her and there is the glint of metal keys in her hand. I push the American out of my way, but my feet are moving too slowly. Sharp jolts of pain pulse through my fingers. I need to slow her down, but she steps into the driving seat and I hear the engine start. I raise my hand to attract her attention as her car begins to move. She brushes her long dark hair from her face and now she sees me waving. She lowers her window and waves cheerfully as she turns towards the cemetery gates and accelerates out on to the road.

I stand rigid on the path. In my pockets my fingers are trembling. They reach for my needles and grip tight around the comforting sharp, cold steel. I know I can find Helena Grigson again. This is just a minor delay. But I am furious I let her slip away so easily. I have everything planned, ready, prepared. I hear footsteps on the path behind me and there's a tap on my shoulder. I turn to see the American Molly Sturlen. She is saying something to me, but now I am no longer listening. I am looking at her thin soft skin, her bulging veins, her red lips stretched wide in a grin. When she is no longer smiling, I predict those lips will be fleshy and soft. Like a pin cushion.

"So, you really want to know about this man?" I ask and her head nods excitedly.

I look away and breathe deeply. "I might have some old photographs somewhere. If you could give me a lift home, I could see if I have anything that would be useful."

We are walking to her car, and my hands are beginning to relax.

My fingers always grow steady when they know, very soon, their craft will begin.

CLARE DORNAN

Clare Dornan writes and directs tv programmes. She works with a lot of presenters of documentaries. In her spare time she escapes the challenges of her day job by conjuring up imaginary characters that do and say exactly what they're told. Her stories have been been performed in and around Bristol and previously published in *North by Southwest* and *The Dark Half of the Year* which got her a mention in Best Horror of the Year 2018.

She's got a Twitter account, @dorny1 which she really must get round to making work. She's also more reliably @clared129 on Instagram.

Gravewatcher

CHRISSEY HARRISON

1

Carina watched from the cemetery gate. Her new arrival tried to shove the gardener's shoulder, passed straight through, and stumbled to his knees. Those who died suddenly always went through a period of confusion. Denial. This one, a young man, wore a dinner jacket, unbuttoned, and a bow tie hung loose over his blood-stained dress shirt.

The blood wasn't real. More an echo of how he'd died.

She needed to catch his attention, but it would be tricky with the gardener there, so she waited. Steam rose from the warm paper cup between her gloved hands. A daily double shot latte had become her morning crutch since sleep began to elude her. Since Maggie died.

The spirit stepped in front of the gardener and waved a hand in front of the man's face. "Hey! Look at me!"

But, the man methodically pushed his mower between the graves, completely oblivious.

The ghost raked his hands through his dark hair, sagged onto a headstone and folded his arms across his chest. Now that he'd calmed down Carina had a better chance of controlling the situation. She tucked a loose curl of hair under her beanie, then strode up the gravel path.

"Good morning, Doug," she called.

The gardener looked up and she raised her coffee cup in greeting.

"Good morning Miss Lewins. Turned a bit fresh today." He carefully manoeuvred the manual mower around a clump of daffodils.

"It certainly has. Still won't let the boss buy you a proper electric mower?"

He chuckled. "Oh no, this is better. Can't be making a racket around the residents." He nodded towards the gravestones.

Carina smiled and when Doug returned his attention to his work she made deliberate eye contact with the young man perched on the headstone. He tensed. She gave a subtle nod towards the rear of the cemetery.

"See you later then," she said.

"You have a pleasant day, Miss Lewins."

As she set off towards the heart of the cemetery the young man hopped up and fell into step beside her. She braced herself for the inevitable hard questions.

"Can you see me?" he asked.

She kept her eyes forward. "Mmm hmm."

"What the hell is going on? Why couldn't he see me? Is this my blood or... I can't remember how I got here."

"It'll come back in time," she said. "I'm afraid you died."

"No, that's not—" He tried to grab her arm and she flinched, even though his hand passed straight through her.

Stay professional.

"Do you remember your name?" she asked.

"Victor." He frowned at his hand. "Victor Mason."

"I know it's difficult to accept, Victor, but you were buried here yesterday afternoon."

He blinked slowly and then looked down at his bloody clothes. "Nah, this is bullshit. Someone's sick joke after the wedding."

Carina hid her reaction by chugging some more of her coffee. She couldn't get caught up in his story; he was just passing through. She schooled her expression and offered a sympathetic smile. "It's true. But it's okay, I'm here to help you."

"If I'm dead, like you say, isn't it a bit late?"

"This isn't the end. When you're ready, you can move on."

"Move on where?"

She gripped the paper cup tighter. "I can't tell you that part."

He curled his lip. "Of course you can't. But I should trust you and everything will be fine? Right. Lady, this is all nuts."

She winced at the scathing bite in his tone.

"Screw this," he said. "Tell whoever put you up to it that I'm not playing." He strode away towards the cemetery gate.

"You can't leave," she called after him.

"Watch me."

She let him go. He'd find her when he was ready and someone else needed her more.

* * *

Towards the south side of the cemetery, pale pink blossom, from a pair of cherry trees, fluttered on the breeze. In the shade beneath the trees, a child huddled beside a grave; her own. Her shoulders trembled with sobs, but her long blonde hair hid her tears. Bare toes peeked out below her soft cotton pyjamas.

Carina paused and finished her coffee. The bottle in her bag whispered to her. Liquid courage. But, no. The caffeine would have to be enough. The bottle was only to help her sleep. If it came to the point where she couldn't get through the days without it, then she was in trouble.

The little girl reached for a teddy bear one of her grieving relatives had placed on the grave. Her small hand passed through, denying her even that small comfort. Spirits couldn't affect any change on the world, and anything living, or 'of the living,' was as insubstantial to them as air.

Carina set her empty cup on the ground beside the path, took off her scarf and gloves, and draped them over a headstone. The child kept her head down as Carina sat cross-legged on the grass beside the grave.

In the five years since she'd first felt the Call, she'd helped too many kids cross over. It never got any easier, but she'd learnt to arm herself with information.

"Hi, Susannah."

The little girl's head snapped up.

"It's okay. I'm here to help."

Susannah blinked big glassy eyes, her cheeks glistening with tears. "Where's my mum?"

"She can't be here right now, sweetheart. I'm sorry."

"I want to go home."

Carina's eyes stung. "I know. But, you can't go home now. You have to go somewhere else. I can show you the way. And when you get there, your grandma's going to take care of you."

"Mummy said Nanny had to go away and can't come back."

"That's right, she did. And now you're going to go there too, to see her. Won't that be nice?"

Susannah wiped her eyes with her sleeve and nodded.

"Are you ready?" Carina held her breath as she extended her hand. Susannah's fingers slid into hers. They felt cool but solid and Carina released the breath. "Good girl. Well done."

She closed her eyes and felt for the ever-present edge of her reality; the veil between the living world and the mystery beyond. She drew back the curtain.

"Nanny!" Susannah sprang to her feet and her hand pulled free.

Carina's arm dropped to her side.

"What did you do to her?" Victor said behind her.

She jumped. The accusation stabbed her raw nerves. She kept her head down and wiped the tears from her cheeks so he wouldn't see. "She did it herself. All I did was open the way."

"The way where?"

"Wherever she's supposed to go. Like I said, I don't control that part."

She rose and returned to the path. He watched her warily, fresh pain in his eyes; he must have tried the gate. She felt for him, but some spirits couldn't be told, they had to learn the hard way.

She held out her hand.

He flinched away from her. "Don't touch me."

"You're right, I'm sorry. When you're ready." She couldn't force him. He'd have to get there on his own. She checked her watch; ten minutes left to visit the others before work.

"Wait, where are you going?" Victor asked.

"Come along and you'll see."

The maze of paths led deeper into the wooded part of the cemetery where grand monuments to the Victorian dead listed and toppled into a sea of ivy. The path dipped towards the Dell—a small clearing where several routes crossed at the base of a steep bank.

"Hey, Gravewatcher," one of Carina's lost souls barked from his perch on the side of a raised tomb. "Have you found my boy yet?"

"Good morning to you too, Mr Tully."

"Bah! What's good about it? It's shit. Like everything else."

"Hey!" Victor said. "What's your problem?"

Mr Tully focused on the new spirit. Carina sighed and moved between them. "Ignore him. He's just a bitter old man who won't let go."

"And what would you know about bitter, Gravewatcher?"

She said nothing. She knew enough.

Mr Tully leaned back. "At least you ain't stuck here."

"Neither are you, George. You can move on any time

you like." She turned her back on him and continued into the middle of the clearing.

"Bah."

Victor trailed along behind her. "What did he mean about finding his son?"

"He doesn't approve of his son's life choices. Wants me to pass on a message."

"And? Will you?"

She stopped and faced him. Hope shone in his eyes. Hope she had to shatter quickly. Cleanly.

"No. I can't."

"But, why not? You could—"

"No I can't. It's not allowed. Like the gate."

He sagged. "Oh."

Around the Dell her little gaggle of lost souls gathered; those who couldn't move on because of some lingering attachment to the living world. One young woman with short, pixie cut dark hair crouched, rocking on her ankles. Another woman, wearing a green satin evening dress, stared up into the trees with a soft sad smile on her lips. A man in biker's leathers sat with his back to a headstone, knees drawn up. He scratched at a patch of bare earth with a finger, leaving no impression.

Half a dozen others loitered among the trees. It would be so much easier if she could act as a medium. Then she could do something to offer them closure.

A matronly spirit named Peggy, hurried towards her.

"Carina dear, have you seen Juliette? I can't find her anywhere."

"Not yet, no. But I'm sure she's around."

It wasn't exactly out of character; Juliette had died

as a teenager, about eight months ago, and her grief for her life was still fresh. She preferred to work through it alone.

Peggy pulled her knitted wrap tighter around her shoulders and glanced at Victor.

"Is something wrong?" Carina asked.

"We heard noises last night. Shrieking."

Carina tried to swallow against a suddenly dry throat. She took several shallow breaths. It was important the spirits saw her as confident; Maggie taught her that very early on.

"Have any of you actually seen anything?" she asked.

Peggy shook her head.

"Well then. It was probably nothing. Don't you think we'd know if there was something here?"

There hadn't been a piece of the Darkness larger than a cat in her cemetery since Maggie defeated the last serious threat. The chances that two would find her spirits in such a short space of time seemed impossibly unlikely. She closed her eyes and tried to will away the tension in her gut.

It had to be nothing. Had to be. She started walking towards the crematorium.

Victor followed her. "Wait, where are you going now?"

Her mind was elsewhere. "What?"

"You're leaving me here?"

She rubbed her eyes. "I have to go to work, I'm sorry. The others will help you."

He frowned, but retreated a pace. She offered an apologetic smile and hurried back toward the land of the living.

2

Victor stood beside the woman in the green dress and stared up into the trees trying to follow her gaze. As far as he could see, there was nothing up there.

That first morning, a week ago, when he'd approached the gate, a painful tingle set in and grew worse with each step closer, until he was gasping through gritted teeth, his whole body on fire. That had really hammered home the point. He was dead.

"She's tapped in the head, that one," barked Mr Tully from where he sat on the edge of a half-buried vault.

Victor glanced up. The old ghost nodded towards the girl in the green dress.

"She's looking for something, I'm sure of it," Victor said. "Won't she be able to move on if she finds it? Maybe we could help look."

Tully guffawed and slapped his thigh. He kept laughing and wiped a finger under his eyes as if they were watering.

Victor scowled. "Why is that funny?"

Tully dropped down and landed with an age defying spring in his knees. "If it were that easy even our green little Gravewatcher could've figured it by now. Nah, you don't get it. If we knew what were holding us here we'd have one foot out the door already. It's the not knowing in itself that keeps us stuck here." He gestured to the girl in the green dress. "Bethany there's been here so long she's lost her marbles."

"So, if we don't figure it out we'll go crazy?"

The old ghost shrugged. "Some do, some don't."

Victor frowned. "But, I thought you knew what your unfinished business was. Carina said you wanted her to contact your son."

"I just like teasing the little Gravewatcher sometimes is all," Tully said with a chuckle. "My boy'll do alright. He has to."

"So, what is your unfinished business?"

He rapped his knuckles on Victor's skull. "You deaf or just plain stupid, boy? I said I don't know. None of us do."

Victor batted his hand away. "But don't you want to figure it out?"

"I's in no rush."

"Why not?"

"I likes the peace and quiet. Besides, she needs someone to look out for her until she toughens up a bit."

Victor stared. "Who?"

"Who do you think? Young Miss Lewins."

Carina had said Tully could leave any time he wanted. Victor narrowed his eyes. "I think she's got you figured out pretty good."

"Bah! She don't know nothing." Tully stomped off.

Victor perched on a headstone. He wouldn't know if he had unfinished business until he tried to cross over, and he wasn't sure which he was more afraid of; staying or going. Hence why he'd avoided Carina all week. The girl in the green dress continued her slow circuit around the Dell. She never spoke. Never reacted. To spend eternity like that would be hell.

Scuffed footsteps accompanied by a rhythmic tapping drew his attention. The Gravewatcher strode towards the Dell along the wide, paved path from the crematorium where she worked, a long walking stick in her right hand.

Victor closed his eyes and took a deep breath—habit rather than necessity. He could hang around and sulk about his death, but what would be the point?

He stood. "Hey."

She glanced up then rubbed her eyes with her free hand.

He trotted over to meet her. "I think I'm ready to give it a go."

"Okay, good." She leaned on her walking stick and extended her left hand.

He hesitated. "If it works, do I have to go through with it now?"

"It'll only work if you do."

He nodded slowly, and then reached for her hand. His fingers phased through hers without a hint of resistance.

"I'm sorry," she said.

"Wait, try it again." He tried to grab her retreating hand, but his fingers closed on thin air.

"It's okay," she said. "Not everyone can move on straight away."

He shoved his fingers into his hair and squeezed his skull. "No. I can't stay here like this. I need to *do* something."

"Just give it a little time."

She walked on. He followed.

In the Dell, Bethany still drifted. Mr Tully and Peggy stood to one side.

Carina leaned her walking stick against a tree. "Where's everyone else?"

"Resting," Peggy said. "It came again last night. We all heard it this time."

Victor hung back, observing. He'd heard the noises too. Somewhere between a bird of prey and a whining cam belt; it had raised the hairs on his neck.

"No sign of Juliette?" Carina asked.

Peggy shook her head. "None. It must have taken her."

"We still don't know that. But, if there is something here I'll take care of it. I'm going to top up the wards right now."

She picked up the walking stick and strode towards a path up the steep, wooded slope towards the rear of the cemetery.

Victor jogged after her. "Can I tag along?"

"If you want. Why?"

"I don't like feeling useless." He shoved his hands in his pockets as they walked side by side. "The others are afraid."

"Yes."

"Why? What's out there? They keep saying the Darkness is coming. What do they mean?"

She sucked her bottom lip like she wasn't sure where to start or how much to say. "The Darkness is... When humans do terrible things—murder, war, hate—they draw the Darkness and give it form. They create monsters that prey on human spirits stuck on this plane."

"And you think there's one here?"

"I don't know, maybe." She stopped beside a grave with an angel monument, propped her walking stick against the surrounding iron railings, and unslung her backpack.

Victor inspected the stick. Fine lines of gold wire, inlaid into the wood, traced intricate patterns, connecting tiny chips of quartz and amethyst like components on a circuit board.

Carina brought out a bundle of sticks and herbs from her bag. She held a lighter to one end until the flame caught hold. Long streamers of smoke that curled towards Victor made his skin tingle.

Carina muttered something.

"What's that?"

"Shh!" she snapped.

He kept his mouth shut and watched as she picked up the walking stick, held it at shoulder height and positioned her fingers over specific crystal chips. The interconnecting gold filaments lit up. She traced a shape with the tip, which hung in the air like the afterglow of a bonfire night sparkler.

The symbol began to fade while she extinguished the herbs and closed up her bag.

"What is that?" Victor asked.

"One of my wards. They keep Darkness at bay."

She started walking again. Victor followed a couple of paces behind.

They visited another four spots around the perimeter of the graveyard while the light faded.

Every time he asked Carina a question she kept her answers short and evasive, which only made him more determined to understand. He'd never liked being a bystander, out of the loop.

They paused in an area peppered with fresh graves, including his own. Carina was tracing the latest ward in the air when a noise like a plunger sucking at a blocked drain made them both flinch. The unfinished ward sputtered and died.

"What was that?" Victor asked.

Carina muttered a few words and the staff glowed bright enough to illuminate a puddle of black, two meters long, as it wormed across the grass.

A violent shiver passed up Victor's spine. He edged sideways, out of its path. The black slug reared up and its pointed nose swayed from side to side. It homed in on him and changed direction.

"Er, Carina? This thing is following me." He backed away.

The Gravewatcher darted in front of him. The shadow creature quivered. Its edges blurred as the light dissolved it like acid, but it kept slugging its oily bulk forward.

"It's okay," Carina said. "Just stay behind me."

She rotated the staff in her hands so the tip pointed down and changed her finger placement so she covered different crystal chips.

"Lancea Longini," she said.

Spidery lines of warm yellow light extended from the staff to form a spearhead around the blunt tip. Carina lanced the black slug with one swift thrust. The Darkness lost cohesion and spread into a bubbling, oil slick pool. With a gurgle like the last of the bathwater draining away, it soaked into the grass.

Carina set the butt of her staff on the ground. "That's that then."

Victor shuddered and rolled his shoulders. "What was that thing?"

"Just a grave leech. They are dangerous but they're slow, so no big deal."

"And that's what took Juliette?" He stared at the spot where the leech had dissolved.

"It must be." She picked up her backpack. "Right, I'm going home. You can find your way back to the Dell, right?"

"I... Okay, sure."

She couldn't possibly believe the leech made the noises they'd heard. It was like she wanted to accept the easy answer. He watched her walk away and frowned. If she was their only line of defence he'd have to keep an eye on her and make sure she did her job.

3

After dealing with the grave leech, Carina avoided the cemetery for as long as she could, but the Call only allowed her a couple of days before she began to feel irritable and uncomfortable. When she returned, she headed straight for the Dell. Each step through the cemetery grounds soothed the unwelcome itch crawling over her skin.

In the clearing at the heart of the cemetery her lost souls gathered. Peggy clucked over the weaker spirits like a mother hen while Tully skulked among the graves muttering to himself. Victor watched over the whole group from a perch on the edge of a vault set into the bank, his expression dark and foreboding.

She cringed; it was selfish to have stayed away so long.

"Oh Carina, thank goodness," Peggy said, hurrying over. "It's Bethany. It took her."

Carina's heart stuttered. She searched the Dell for the girl in the green satin dress. Bethany was always there. She'd always been there, since before Carina received the Call. "But I—When?"

"Last night. We saw it this time and—"

"It weren't no bloomin' grave leech or hollow rat!" Tully barked. "It were big."

She shook her head. "No. Listen to yourselves. It's just fear talking, blowing things out of proportion."

"Are we?" Victor said. "Are you sure it's not you who's afraid?"

Her chest tightened and she wiped her eyes with her sleeve. His words stripped away the lies she'd been telling herself. She had a duty to protect them, no matter how much it scared her, and she'd already let whatever was out there take two of her spirits.

She met his gaze across the clearing and his expression softened. He blinked and his lips parted as if he wanted to say something, but then he looked away.

"It's okay," she said. "I'm not going to let anything else happen."

Victor jumped down from the tomb. "Can we help?"

"You'll only be safe if you cross over so the best thing you can do is work on that."

She ran her hands over the crystal bumps and gold lines of her staff to ground herself. If felt like only yesterday Maggie had coached her through making it as part of her early training, and yet the nine months since Maggie died stretched out forever.

She toured the graveyard again, topped up the wards, again, and chased a few hollow rats out of a crypt. The Shadow vermin didn't pose much threat individually, but they could multiply if left unchecked.

There was no sign of anything larger.

By two in the morning her limbs were growing heavy and her eyes itched. The bitter wind nipped at her cheeks and found every way in through her coat and hoodie. She blew into her hands and rubbed them together.

"I'd offer you my jacket," Victor said. "But incorporeal, so..." He shrugged.

He'd been following her around all evening, which had forced her to keep up an exhausting front of composure. She wished he would go away so she could find a quiet spot to work through the paralysing fear alone, and maybe steal a nip from the bottle in her bag to steady her nerves.

"Do you think my unfinished business might be how I died?" Victor asked. "Is it weird that I still can't remember what happened?"

"It's not unusual," she said. "But I doubt that's what's

holding you here."

"I can't stop thinking how it must have hurt them. Right after the wedding."

She glanced over. She should keep her distance, but his perpetual presence made it hard not to give in to curiosity, and she could use the distraction. "Your wedding?"

He shook his head. "My sister's. What if I did something stupid and it was my fault? It was supposed to be a happy day for her and now my death will always cast a shadow. Maybe I'm supposed to make amends or something."

She leaned on her staff. "Victor, you're dead. There's nothing you can do to make amends. Ever."

His face fell. "I know. It's just... I wish there was a way I could know whether they were coping. If I knew how it happened then maybe—"

Carina sighed. "I'm sorry. You're right—Of course you need to know. I'll see what I can find out."

"Thank you."

A piercing wail shattered the silence and echoed through the cemetery. Her limbs froze and she almost dropped the staff.

"What is it? Do you recognise it?"

She nodded and crouched, holding her staff so tight the crystal chips dug into her palms as she scanned the undergrowth and the forest canopy. "Did you hear where it came from?"

"No."

Another shriek made her jump. This time it had definitely come from behind, towards the Dell where the other lost souls were.

"Come on, we have to hurry!" She broke into a run. A few moments later she burst into the clearing.

Peggy herded the weaker spirits into a group, trying to shield them, while George Tully faced the advancing Shadow.

"Come on then, beasty!" he yelled. "You think I'm scared of you? I ain't scared of nothing!" The spirit held his fists up as if he could punch the Darkness.

"George, don't!" Carina called. The demonic form closing in on Tully obscured the treetops. Too black to be real, it hurt her eyes to look at it.

A Mort-Tan-Gar: The Death Shadow of War. Spawned from the worst atrocities. Composed of the darkness found at the bottom of abyssal trenches. It morphed as it moved, one moment completely fluid, the next harshly solid. A black tendril extended and sharpened into a clawed hand.

Carina placed trembling fingers over a set of crystals at either end of the staff and held it above her head for *Heaven's Wall.*

"Qir muggin," she cried in her best approximation of the ancient Hebrew incantation. She swiped the staff down like closing a shutter.

A foot in front of Tully the Mort-Tan-Gar's claw crashed into a barrier, which flared bright white. The beast shrieked and recoiled. Slanted eyes like hot coals fixed on her.

"Gravewatcher." Its voice rumbled like distant earthquakes.

The staff in Carina's hands shook violently where she

still held it out across her body. She swung it down so she held the butt and set her fingers for *Michael's Blade.*

"Gladio Caerulum!" The gossamer shape of a sword formed around the staff, traced in a web of blue flame. It was posturing, to give herself confidence. Only *The Light of a Thousand Suns* could destroy a Mort-Tan-Gar.

Or *The Immolation.*

The Darkness drew back a clubbed fist the size of a small car and swung for the barrier. Carina's spell shattered into a thousand diamond shards and the creature charged.

She caught a blur of motion out the corner of her eye as Victor lunged towards her, but his spirit form passed straight through her. She dropped to her knees with the sword held above her head. The Shadow pulled up, sailed overhead and disappeared into the night.

"Are you okay?" Victor asked as he picked himself up.

Carina rubbed her eyes. Bright after images of the shattered barrier spell filled her vision. She was still alive, for now, but she was so very far from okay.

She rounded on him. "What were you thinking?"

He stepped back.

"There is nothing you can do except get yourself destroyed. Is that what you want?"

"I didn't—"

"Stay out of my way, do you understand?"

He blinked at her, jaw working though no words formed.

She looked around at the other lost souls. Peggy shepherded her charges from the side of the Dell.

Tully joined them. "Pretty light show there,

Gravewatcher. Not bad."

"Better than challenging it to fisticuffs. You're worse than him!" She nodded towards Victor.

Tully rolled his eyes. "Well I ain't one to go down without a fight is all."

"Do you think it will come back?" Peggy asked.

"Yes. I don't think it was expecting me but that won't keep it away for long."

The girl with the pixie haircut tipped her head back and let out a keening cry, making them all jump. Carina quickly counted the spirits and came up one short.

"Where's Joey?"

The spirits exchanged frightened glances. Joey Jenkins—the man in the biker's leathers. Gone.

Carina squeezed her fist by her side. "I need to move you all on. Now. You can't stay here. It's not safe."

"You know it's not that easy," Victor said.

"Of course I know that! But we have to try, otherwise—"

"You can fight it. I know you can."

She glared at him. "You have no idea what you're saying. You don't know anything. I can't—Stop pretending like you care and leave me alone." She stormed straight through him and ran before the tears could start.

4

Tully threw his hands up. "Well, shit."

Victor's gut cramped with an uncomfortable mix

of guilt and frustration. Maybe he didn't know what he was talking about but he knew one thing; she was braver than she gave herself credit for. When she'd heard the shriek she'd raced towards the danger without hesitation.

"Poor lass," Peggy said. "I hope she's up to it." She held the girl with the pixie cut hair, stroking her back as the spirit sobbed against her shoulder.

"How long have you been here?" Victor asked her.

"Oh, about ten years, give or take."

"So you've seen her face things like that before, right?"

"Oh no, not like that. Only ever seen one like that, and Maggie Hobbs took care of that one."

When the spirits had mentioned Maggie Hobbs before, it had been in the awed tone of legend, which left him with the impression she been gone a long time. Suddenly he wasn't so sure.

"What happened to her?"

Peggy shrugged. "We don't really know. Other than she didn't make it through the fight. Carina doesn't much like to talk about it."

In the short time he'd known her he'd come to realise that Carina didn't much like to talk about things full stop. Or maybe it was just the spirits she kept at arm's length.

He paced away from the others. He shouldn't be concerning himself with Carina at all. She would have to handle the monster alone no matter how much he wanted to help, and he needed to figure out his unfinished business.

The problem was there were a million things he'd

wanted to do with his life. Finish his Master's degree. Get his dream job. See the world. Now he'd never compete with his pentathlon team again. His little sister's family would grow up minus an uncle. He'd never fall in love again.

How was he supposed to pick out which one meant more than anything else?

He stared down the path where Carina had stormed off. Maybe the first step would be to stop adding to the list.

Following her was pointless. There was nothing he could do, and she clearly didn't want his moral support, but he couldn't do nothing. It was in his nature to protect, it always had been, to the point of fault; not everyone needed or wanted saving. He'd learnt that through painful experience.

Death had simultaneously presented him with someone in need and stripped him of all capacity to act. If he had to come to terms with *that* before he could move on then he was going to be stuck here for a very long time.

5

Carina spent the rest of the night hiding from the lost souls, wandering paths of the cemetery that she knew like home, but which grew hostile and unfamiliar in the dark. As the first threads of dawn coloured the sky pink she gravitated towards one particular grave.

Fresh, vibrant tulips filled the vase in front of the headstone. Maggie Hobbs had children, grandchildren, nieces and nephews, and they kept the grave pristine. She was well loved and missed, but none of her family ever knew about her other life. They didn't know about Carina and how Maggie had saved her when the Call threatened to drive her mad.

She set her backpack and staff down and knelt on the damp grass at the side of her mentor's resting place. Tears filled her eyes.

When the Call stole her life, kept her distant from the living and exposed her to the Darkness, Maggie Hobbs offered the warmth of human comfort. She'd been more than a teacher; she'd been the only friend Carina could confide in.

"I don't know if I can be brave like you."

From her backpack she pulled out a battered leather-bound book, inherited from Maggie. Her handbook, of sorts. She leafed through to a page which depicted an intricate sequence of hand holds, motions, shapes to trace, words to speak. *The Light of a Thousand Suns.* The gravewatchers' ultimate weapon, but it took time. Even with forty years' experience, and Carina trying everything to slow the Darkness down, Maggie hadn't pulled it off.

It was a false promise. False hope.

She turned to the last page in the book where an illustration showed a gravewatcher kneeling with a sword of blue fire clasped in her hands—*Michael's Blade*—used as a conduit. The figure herself shone with an inner light.

The Immolation.

The spell consumed the gravewatcher's soul and turned it into an explosion of light powerful enough to destroy even the strongest piece of Darkness. That was how Maggie had defeated the last one and her family had no idea her spirit wouldn't be waiting for them on the other side.

"You promised I wouldn't have to," Carina whispered as tears rolled down her cheeks. "You said it was once in a lifetime."

Some days she didn't feel she had much to live for. She existed apart from the living world, as if a second veil separated her from real life. The Call tethered her to the graveyard, restricting her ability to travel, to live, to love.

But she wasn't ready to die. Worse: to cease to exist.

She flicked the book's pages and they fell open on an illustration of an indistinct figure in plate armour holding a blue sword. A suggestion of wings fanned out behind him. Michael. The original guardian.

But, guardians were myth; warriors from the spirit world, from a distant time when the power that ruled beyond the veil still cared about the living world.

Carina wiped her eyes. If there were any other way then Maggie would still be with her. She reached for the bottle in her bag and unscrewed the cap.

"Carina?"

She flinched and stuffed the bottle back into the backpack, then glanced over her shoulder. Victor stood a pace behind her, eyes fixed on where the bag gaped open.

"What do you want?" she asked, trying to keep her voice level.

"I wanted to see how you were holding up. Not great I see." He nodded towards the bottle.

"It's not what you think."

He sat beside her. "So you're not drinking hard spirits at five in the morning?"

"It's just to help me sleep sometimes."

"Then why do you carry it with you?"

"I don't. I just didn't unpack it." The lump in her throat made it hard to speak. "And I'm fine. So you can go."

She dipped her head, so he wouldn't see she'd been crying, but he leaned closer, trying to see, and she couldn't twist far enough. Her chest tightened and she snapped round to face him.

"What do you want me to say? Yes, I was going to have a drink because I thought it might make dying easier. That's how scared I am. So can you please just leave me alone!" She picked up the bottle and flung it through him. It landed on the grass and ebbed amber rum into the soil.

Victor leaned back. "I'm sorry, I didn't mean..."

She tried to stand up, but her shoes slipped on the damp grass and she crashed back onto her knees with one arm out in front of her. All the strength left her. She wanted to curl up into a ball until it was over.

"It's okay to be scared," Victor said. "You don't have to pretend you're not."

Carina stared at the grass in front of her. "Yes I do."

"Why?"

"Because if I stop pretending, I won't go through with

it."

He shifted to sit with his knees drawn up, facing her. "Go through with what?"

She glanced at the quiet concern in his eyes, open and raw, and suddenly it was too much effort to resist his persistent onslaught on the walls she'd put up.

She slumped onto her hip. "I never asked to be what I am, but I thought I'd accepted it. I even started to enjoy parts of it. Now I have to give up everything because if I don't, the Darkness will destroy you all."

She ran her hand over the ridges and crystal points of her staff where it lay in the grass beside her.

Victor leaned forward with his hands clasped between his knees. "What do you mean everything?"

"I mean everything. My life, my soul. Everything."

"Then don't," he said. "I would never ask you to die for me. Neither would the others, if they knew."

He reached out as if he wanted to touch her arm but stopped short and clenched his fist. "We're not worth your life."

Her eyes filled with more tears. "It's alright. It's just what I have to do. My duty. My choice, not yours."

"No. I—Come on, there has to be another way."

"Only a miracle."

"What kind of miracle?"

She touched the aged parchment pages of the book between them. "Time."

The Mort-Tan-Gar didn't return immediately and waiting to die was insufferable. On the basis that false hope trumped no hope, Carina distracted herself with practice.

In the Dell, glowing sigils hung in the air in a hemisphere around her. As she filled in the final gap the air crackled with expectation. She stood with her feet braced and raised the staff towards the tree she was using as a target. The symbols flared. Like the antenna in the middle of a satellite dish, the staff channelled their energy and light burst from the tip. The staff kicked back in her hands with the force and the beam blasted the tree.

She quickly released her grip and the spell faded leaving a blinding afterimage.

"Well?" she asked Victor.

He stood peering down at her phone where it sat on a nearby headstone timing her.

"Three minutes twenty."

She threw one hand up in the air. "Oh, that's ridiculous. That's slower!" She marched over to the phone and reset the timer. One more.

She took up her position opposite the scorched tree and tried to clear her mind. Holding her staff horizontally at arm's length in front of her she moved first one end, then the other, in a small circle. The ends of the staff left trails of gold in the air. As she moved, she murmured words in Hebrew, Latin and other languages—some she didn't even know the names of—full of archaic, guttural vowels.

She'd memorised the spell with Maggie a long time ago, but she'd never pushed herself to see how fast she could be. She kept her motions tight, her voice clipped, rushing through each element. Done in a controlled way, *The light of a Thousand Suns* more closely resembled a dance than a spell, but when trying to shave every fraction of a second down it lost its elegance.

That was okay. She didn't need elegant, she needed fast. She braced herself for the recoil, thrust, and—nothing.

"Shit."

"Three minutes dead," Victor said from behind her. "But I think you missed part of that second incantation again."

"Oh, what do you know?"

He held his hands up. "Just trying to help."

"Sorry. You're right." She rubbed her eyes.

For a while she'd let herself believe in the false promise the spell offered. Deluded herself that she could force a third option that didn't require her life. She had improved, but there was a limit to the gains she could make before the spell became unreliable. She needed to stop pretending, but thinking about *The Immolation* led only towards a dark void of terror. At least the practice kept her mind occupied. She re-set the timer and took up the first position again.

It didn't help that she was exhausted. She couldn't leave the cemetery unattended at night and sleep didn't come easily at the best of times. Trying to snatch a few hours before and after work, while it was still daylight, wasn't working.

She half wished the Mort-Tan-Gar would hurry up, because if she had to go much longer without a proper night's sleep she'd welcome death.

She reached the end of the spell, stabbed the staff forward and smote the tree with *The Light of a Thousand Suns.*

"Three minutes fifteen," Victor said.

She rubbed her eyes and yawned.

"Maybe you should take a break," he said.

Every second she was in the cemetery he was there, like her shadow. But, since their talk beside Maggie's grave she hadn't felt the need to pretend around him. They'd spent a lot of the dark hours of the night talking. She'd opened up about her life, her fears, dreams, regrets, and when it became too much, and she broke down crying, he would sit close and tell her silly stories from when he was alive until she laughed.

She'd miss him when he crossed over, but she had to try to help.

"I brought something for you," she said.

"Yeah?"

"Yeah. You ready to know how you died?"

6

Carina walked over to where she'd left her backpack and pulled out a sheaf of paper.

Victor hesitated. The contents of that paper could unlock a way out he wasn't sure he wanted to take any more.

She watched him expectantly. "Well?"

"Okay." It wouldn't work unless he chose it anyway.

She sat down and spread the papers on the ground. He sat beside her.

"It was a car accident," she said. "You were driving but you weren't over the limit or anything."

He scanned the photocopied newspaper articles. A lorry had lost control. "Was anyone else killed?"

"No. There was a passenger. He survived."

Victor closed his eyes as flashes returned to him.

Condensation. Windscreen wipers on full. His friend, Paul, turning the radio up over the noise from the rain. Brake lights fractured through the droplets. Truck tyres screeching.

The windscreen shattered as something lanced through the glass. Pain in his chest like nothing he'd ever experienced.

He shook his head and clutched at the blood stain on his shirt.

"So now you know." Carina said.

"Yeah."

She held her hand out. "Do you want to try?"

He quickly snatched his hands behind his back and she frowned at him.

"Maybe later. You should practice some more."

She glanced over at her staff. "Okay. But you will try later, right? I'd rather know you were safe."

"But you'll still be here."

"Vic, we already know what's going to happen to me. Only one of us has to die."

He smiled. "I'm already dead, remember?"

She scowled. "You know what I mean."

* * *

A small campfire burned in a ring of stones in the Dell. The gravewatcher hunched in the lee of a mausoleum, her coat zipped up tight, a blanket wrapped round her legs. Her head lolled on her shoulder as she dozed.

Victor sat close beside her. The dying fire needed more wood, but he couldn't add any. He couldn't do anything to help and the frustration ate him up inside.

He watched the firelight flicker over her features. She was going to die, and the universe was going to make him watch. It wasn't fair. She had the strength and the courage to fight, but the game was rigged and there was nothing either of them could do to change that.

Maybe this was Hell. His Hell.

"I wish I could give you a fair chance. If there was anything I could do, even if it meant the end of me. I'm dead already. You shouldn't have to..." He swallowed against the lump in his throat and tipped his head back to gaze at the few stars visible through the tree tops. "A chance, that's all. That's not a lot to ask for, is it?"

Carina's shoulders relaxed. She slowly slumped sideways. Victor tensed, expecting her to fall right through him, but instead her head pressed softly against his shoulder.

He turned his head slowly. "Uh, Carina?"

"Mmm," she mumbled.

For the briefest time he'd felt he was at least half way ready to let go of the world. But, whatever his unfinished business had been, she was what held him here now.

He reached to stroke her hair.

A screech rent the air. Carina's head snapped up and she fell through him. He scrambled out of the way.

She rubbed her eyes and groped for her staff.

"You can do this," he said.

Her eyes connected with his. She nodded and pushed to her feet.

7

The shrieks of the Mort-Tan-Gar circled the Dell. Carina turned on the spot, trying to track it. Victor stood behind her with his back to hers.

"George?" she called.

"Everyone accounted for," Tully replied from the other side of the Dell. Good. She wasn't prepared to lose another spirit tonight.

The monster's cries abruptly ceased. In the sudden silence, Carina's ears roared with rushing blood.

"Do you see it?" she whispered.

"Not yet," Victor said over his shoulder.

"Gravewatcher." The deep, gravel voice made them both flinch. "We know who you are now. The Darkness whispers of you, welp. The child apprentice who let her master die." It chuckled. "No hiding behind mother's skirts this time."

"Show yourself!" Carina yelled. She widened her stance and gripped the staff tight in both hands, poised for *Heaven's Wall*.

The Darkness flowed from every deep shadow in the Dell, pooled in front of them and swelled. She and Victor tilted their heads back as the Mort-Tan-Gar towered over them. Her knees shook.

"Vic, go. It'll destroy you."

"I'm not going anywhere."

The Darkness throbbed with a deep chuckle. "Little guard dog needs to learn he has no teeth, Gravewatcher."

"Please, Vic!" She tried to shove him away with her elbow but of course she couldn't make contact. "Please! Go!"

The Mort-Tan-Gar laughed again and then surged forward.

"Qir muggin," Carina said, firmly drawing her hands down. The Shadow slammed into her bright wall of power and stopped. She immediately took up the first position of *The Light of a Thousand Suns*.

"You've got this," Victor said.

She nodded. Without taking her eyes off the monster, she whipped through the first motions and words—fast, precise—but no more than half the sigils hung in the air when the barrier spell failed. The Darkness boiled towards her.

"No!" Victor shoved her to the ground as the Mort-Tan-Gar swiped a smoke hand tipped with obsidian claws.

Wind ruffled her hair as it missed by inches. She hit the ground hard, rolled away and looked up. The huge black claw closed around Victor and lifted him from the ground.

"No!"

"Run!" he yelled.

The Darkness engulfed him. She stared at the spot where he'd disappeared and couldn't breathe. Somehow he'd touched her. That wasn't possible.

The Mort-Tan-Gar bellowed, so loud her bones vibrated. Her courage failed and she bolted along the path.

The Darkness suffused Victor with a cold so absolute it numbed his body—if he could call it that—until he felt nothing. As it closed over him he wondered, briefly, whether Carina made it away. It might be worth ceasing to exist, if it meant she survived. Then the cold stilled the very thoughts in his mind.

For some indefinable time—maybe seconds, maybe millennia—he was nothing.

Then came light.

And pain.

Tendrils of black smoke clawed at Carina's ankles as her feet pounded the path. Tears streamed down her cheeks. She'd had one chance to stop it. She should have done what was necessary, but she'd deluded herself that she had a fighting chance and because of that Victor was gone.

Brambles and twigs snagged her clothes and behind her the Mort-Tan-Gar's shrill cry ripped through the night.

The chapel and crematorium emerged into view through the trees. She ran for them. The cold air tore at her throat and her lungs burned.

She clattered under the front porch and tried the door but it was locked. With a yelp she spun to face the

Shadow behind her and found nothing but the deserted car park. She pressed her back against the door. A pale porch light glowed above her head. A moth bumped against the plastic casing.

Her breath slowly returned to normal and she slumped down.

She'd left them. Her spirits. Her responsibility. She'd abandoned them.

"Gravewatcher," the rusty voice of the Mort-Tan-Gar wound through the empty graveyard, simultaneously miles away and right behind her.

She drew in a sharp breath, wiped her eyes and stood. The staff quivered in her grip.

Shadows seeped through the bushes, slunk around the corners of the building, closing in on her.

Victor hit the ground face down, hard enough to knock the breath from his lungs. Gasping, he pushed to his knees. His fingers sank into the loam and he scrunched the leaf litter. Cold. Damp.

His shoulders and back ached like crazy.

He sat on his ankles and nearly toppled backwards.

Out the corner of his eye he caught a flash of dirty white and flinched. An unfamiliar weight dragged at his back and threw off his balance.

His hand came down on something cold and hard. He brushed the leaves away. Pale blue flames licked the long bright metal blade of a sword, but gave off no heat. Gingerly, he curled his fingers around the hilt. The flames wrapped around his hand and wrist and suffused his arm with an energy that hummed through his whole body.

A figure approached through the trees.

"Well I'll be damned," George Tully said, slowing to a halt in front of him. "Thought you were a goner for sure."

Victor staggered to his feet. The weight on his back shifted and made him stumble sideways. He turned on the spot.

"Here, watch where you're waving them things."

"What?" He craned his neck to look over his shoulder. Feathers shifted. A dart of panic gripped him.

Then a piercing shriek reminded him where and when he was.

The Mort-Tan-Gar.

Carina.

He glanced back at Tully.

"Well go on then! Before it's too late. Don't worry about us, we'll be fine." Behind him the other spirits huddled together with Peggy.

Bright flashes lit up the night, guiding him to the battle. He set off at a run.

Carina's latest barrier shattered and she fell on her backside as the Darkness swiped at her. She scuttled backwards until she could find her feet, then threw up another wall. She could keep this up half the night, but it would be a stalemate. Pointless.

Instead of taking up the first position for *The Light of a Thousand Suns*, she set her grip for *Michael's Blade*.

The blue outline of the sword formed. She dropped to her knees with the blade point down in front of her, forehead resting on the wooden staff within. Tears dripped off her nose.

She forced out the first syllables of *The Immolation* in a whisper.

"No," grumbled the Darkness. "You're not strong enough to sacrifice yourself."

Where her hand held the staff her skin began to radiate. Heat welled up inside her core. She couldn't close her eyes; the sight of the shadow was the only thing giving her the courage to keep going.

The Mort-Tan-Gar's indistinct smoky form sharpened and it charged, shattering her last barrier. A Shadow fist wrapped around her. One obsidian claw sliced her upper arm, but she kept chanting. The light radiating from her singed the dark flesh of the beast and its grip loosened.

She locked eyes with the Darkness.

Bitter triumph.

A flash of pale blue sailed through the air and cleaved through the Shadow's wrist. The Mort-Tan-Gar howled and retreated across the car park. The severed hand dispersed, flowing back into the recesses under bushes and rocks.

Something wrenched her staff from her hands and her concentration broke.

"No!" she cried. Her skin still radiated but she could already feel the heat inside ebbing away.

"No, no, no. Carina? You can stop now." It sounded like Victor's voice, but it couldn't be. He was gone.

Someone crouched in front of her. Something metallic

clattered on the tarmac. Hands gripped her shoulders.

"Tell me you can make it stop, please."

As the light from her core faded slightly she could see clearer. Victor's face came into focus.

"Are you okay?" he asked.

She pressed her hand to his chest. He felt solid, the fabric of his shirt smooth to her touch. She traced her fingers down the silk bow tie that still hung round his neck. "How are you here?"

He shifted his shoulders. Feathers rustled and she refocused on the wings splaying out from his back.

"Guardian," she whispered. The fog clouding her mind cleared and reality slammed back into her. She clasped her hand to the wound on her arm and gritted her teeth against the sharp pain. Across the car park the Mort-Tan-Gar gather itself and slowly advanced.

"You're—you're my time." Her miracle. Maggie had been right all along. She didn't have to sacrifice herself. The power behind the veil had sent her what she needed. She looked skyward. "I'm sorry I thought you didn't care."

She picked up her staff and levered herself to her feet. "You have to hold it off," she said to Victor as he recovered his sword.

He grinned at her. "Three minutes twenty, right? You've got it."

His feathers brushed her back as he stepped forward. He spread his wings to their full fifteen-foot span and pointed the fiery blade at the Darkness.

"Who's toothless now!" he yelled.

The Mort-Tan-Gar's slanted red eyes glowered down

at him.

Carina widened her stance and held her staff level in steady hands. She circled one end, then the other, leaving a trail of gold hanging in the air.

The Mort-Tan-Gar slashed at Victor and he dove for the ground. The Shadow sailed over him, ruffling the feathers of his new wings.

The sword had a life of its own; he intuitively knew where it wanted to move. He sprang to his feet and lunged at a black tentacle snaking across the car park towards Carina. The beast shrieked. The severed tentacle melted into the ground but another rope of black slithered round his waist, jerked him backwards and tossed him high into the air. Newly implanted instinct kicked in. He fanned his wings just before he hit the ground and somehow landed on his feet.

His attention on the fall, he didn't see the clubbed fist of solid black until it smashed into him. He hit the ground on his back this time and pain tore through his right wing.

He lashed out. The tip of his sword caught the retreating fist, ripping open a trail of smoke which frittered away on the breeze. He rolled to his knees.

The Mort-Tan-Gar advanced on Carina where half her spell now hovered in the air around her. With his right wingtip trailing on the ground Victor chased it down. He slashed, opening a wide rip in the monster's back, but it kept advancing on the Gravewatcher. He needed to get in front of it.

Wincing from the pain in his wing he crouched, leapt, beat hard against the air and rose over the monster. He dropped with the point of the sword aimed down. The Shadow shrank away from the blade. He drove it back a couple of paces and landed hard on the tarmac.

The Mort-Tan-Gar roared and stretched towards Carina. Victor cleaved the reaching tendril, threw his shoulder into the densest part and thrust the sword in deep. All he had to do was hold it.

Carina fluidly scribed the air with gold lines and the incantations flowed from her lips like a song. She didn't rush. Victor would buy her the time she needed, or he wouldn't, but if *she* failed it would all be for nothing.

She slotted the last sigil into place, completing the hemisphere, which sparked and hummed. Setting her feet to absorb the recoil, she aimed.

"Down!" she yelled.

Victor glanced over his shoulder at her. His eyes widened and he dropped flat with his hands over the back of his head.

The sigils funnelled their energy into the staff and *The Light of a Thousand Suns* burst forth. She strained to hold steady. The beam stripped away the outer layers of the Shadow and punched a ragged hold through the denser core. The Darkness instantly unravelled into a thousand smaller entities which fled into the night.

She released her hold and blinked her vision clear.

There would be a tomorrow.

Victor groaned. She rushed to his side as he knelt.

Blood seeped from a graze on his forehead and more stained the feathers of one wing.

"I never thought it would feel so good to hurt," he said.

She grinned at him. "We did it."

"*You* did it. Gravewatcher."

She stood and offered him her hand. He hesitated, then took hold and she helped him to his feet. They stood close and she studied his face. He looked so much more vibrant. His eyes were blue where they'd looked grey before, his skin pinker, hair more brown than black. More alive.

Was he alive? She was going to have to re-read the book for all those passages she'd skipped over about Guardians.

She realised she was still holding his hand and quickly let go. "We should check on the others."

"Yeah." Victor shoved his hand in his pocket and they started walking. After a few paces he stopped. Carina paused further along the path.

"What's wrong?"

He slowly withdrew his hand from his pocket holding a piece of paper. She walked back as he unfolded it.

"I think this is for you," he said, handing it over.

She took it and read the familiar hand writing.

There are no endings, only different types of beginning.
Choose yours. I will see you again.

Maggie.

CHRISSEY HARRISON

Chrissey writes varied speculative fiction and romance, flagrantly defying the usual advice to stick to one genre. She's been learning the craft for nearly ten years in which time her short stories have appeared in several fiction and comic book anthologies including *The Dark Half of The Year*, *Age of Savagery* and *Shock Value (Green)*.

She self-published her 'novellette' *The Star Coin Prophesy in* 2012 to explain why the world didn't end as predicted. Her first novel, *Mime*, sees a paranormal journalists take on a demon mime artist.

Chrissey is a member of the Alliance of Independent Authors, and a supporter of small press and local book stores. When not at her day job or writing she is usually making something weird or cute, or both.

As a co-founder of Great Escape Films, she has also produced independent short and feature films, most recently *Carnival Of Sorrows*.

Find her at chrisseyharrison.com or on Twitter @ChrisseyWrites.

Work Experience

JON CHARLES

MONDAY

I love it here. I love being outdoors. I love the independence. And I love being surrounded by dead people.

I didn't ask to come here, but I never sent the form back for anywhere else. Dad said he'd get me work experience at the BBC but that never happened; like lots of stuff with Dad. So, school arranged for me to come to this cemetery. I think they saw it as a kind of sanction for me being an under-achiever. Some of the other kids made fun of me. Some thought it was a weird place to be sent. The Goth girls were jealous. Mostly, they were too busy going on about wherever they were going to even ask me what I was doing. I don't care. This suits me. The people are nice—Mr North and even Old Jock—and don't go telling me what to do all the time.

Mr North met me at the start of the day and showed me around. He introduced me to the ladies who run the tea shop, saying they were the most important people there and to make sure I was polite to them. One of them, Brenda, asked Mr North what I was going to be doing. He told her I would be doing some clearing and tidying up in the overgrown part of the cemetery. She said something about minding out for Old Jock. Brenda laughed and I noticed Mr North rolling his eyes.

Mr North took me to the area where he wanted me to work and said I seemed like a bright enough lad so he'd leave me to it. After I'd been pulling up weeds for an hour or so Old Jock came down between some trees and introduced himself. He helped me carry the pulled weeds to a compost pile.

TUESDAY

Mr North told me how pleased he was with all the work I'd done the day before. He said they'd never had a better work experience person before. I said my teachers would never believe him.

I carried on clearing the growth away from the old gravestones. I got a sense of accomplishment from uncovering graves that had been hidden for years. After each one was cleared I'd try and see if I could read the words. Some were too faded or had been damaged by plant roots, but sometimes you could make out what had been carved. I liked to read how the dead person had been loved by those they left behind. I wondered if my family would use words like that for me.

Mr North came by occasionally and told me I was doing well. In the middle of the morning I went to the tea shop where Brenda gave me a cup of tea and didn't charge me. She said I'd earned it, from what Mr North had told her. I told her Old Jock had helped me. She laughed and said something about me catching on quickly.

In the afternoon Old Jock came and said hello. This time he asked me if I'd like to have a go at doing some grave digging. I told him I didn't realise that the cemetery still had new burials; it all looked so old and full. He said they only did a few now and just for people who'd had some special connection to the cemetery. He showed me how to measure out the plot and which tools to use for the topsoil and which to use for the harder ground below. I asked him who the grave was for but he said he didn't know yet.

Wednesday

Before I got to the cemetery I met Alya from school. Normally she doesn't talk to me, but this morning she seemed quite friendly. She said she was doing her work experience at a beauty shop just down the road but she didn't like it because they kept going on at her about taking her headscarf off. Alya's family are Albanian Muslims. She never wears the scarf at school but she said she had worn it the first morning to be smart and had decided to keep wearing it after they made a thing out of it. She has nice hair but I agree that it should be up to her what she wears. I told her how much I liked the cemetery and she said she might walk up in her lunch hour to have a look.

One of the graves I uncovered in the morning was for a girl who was born in 1872 but died in 1887 of consumption. I don't know what that is but it made me sad to think of someone the same age as me dying. Who was she? What did she do? The grave had no clues and nor did I.

I sat on one of the benches to eat my sandwiches when Alya walked up and asked if she could join me. We sat next to each other, not saying much to begin with, just eating our lunches. I asked her if she would like me to get her a mug of tea from the shop but she said she had water with her. Alya said she liked the peacefulness of the cemetery. She asked if I would mind if she could come and have lunch with me again tomorrow. I said I didn't mind. Obviously.

In the afternoon I helped Old Jock some more with the fresh grave. He told me he had seen me sitting with Alya and that he thought she was very pretty and looked full of life. I didn't know what to say after that.

Thursday

Alya came and had her lunch with me again. Brenda came over and gave us both mugs of tea. I think she wanted to meet Alya so she could tease me later. I didn't mind.

Miss Hastings from school came to visit. She said she'd spoken to Mr North and he had said how well I was doing. She stood on the path talking to me from a distance. Maybe she didn't want to let her high heels sink in the mud or maybe she was one of those people who gets weird around gravestones. I told her about the grave digging I'd been doing with Old Jock and she looked surprised. I showed her the direction where Old Jock usually came from and she stepped off the path and picked her way through the trees to see if she could find him. She must have found out enough to fill in the form she had with her as I didn't see her again that day. I guessed that she has gone off to visit the next student on her list.

Friday

I was working a few feet from one of the paths in the morning when one of the guided tours came past. The guide stopped and started telling the group about an old legend that said this part of the cemetery was haunted by a spirit that refused to pass on. He told them the legend said that the spirit used to buy extra years of life from 'death' by taking the bodies and souls of those who left the main paths. And always those who should have lived many more years. He said that people used to call the spirit Old Jock. I dropped my tools and ran all the way down the road to the beauty shop where Alya was. It was okay. She was there and gave me a funny look. I realised how it looked for me to turn up there at 11 in the morning and out of breath. I apologised and said I wanted to ask her if she was going to come for lunch again today. She said she was.

After lunch I went to find the grave I'd helped dig. It was filled in and covered in grass and weeds so you couldn't see there had been a grave there at all. The grass and weeds looked like they hadn't been cut back in years.

The police cars arrived after that. They wanted to know when I'd last seen Miss Hastings so I told them. I heard them talking to each other about how they had to check here even though her car had been found next to some cliffs miles away. I wondered how Old Jock had done that.

While I was standing around waiting to see if the police were going to ask me any more questions Alya came walking up. It was five o'clock. End of work experience week. I told Alya I would miss the cemetery. She said we could come back and visit and walk around. Yes, I said, but only if we kept to the paths and she stayed close. She raised her eyebrow and laughed.

"Of course," she said.

JON CHARLES

Jon Charles is a writer of dark fiction which he sends out into the world from his hidden lair in North Bristol. His stories can also be found in *Terror Tree: The Pun Book of Horror Stories, Forever Hungry* and other anthologies. More stories and a novel are on the way.

Angel

Louise Gethin

We met when Zoe ran off, refusing to come back even though I shouted her name over and over. I took her for walks most days in the summer after school, and at weekends. She'd never run off before.

I searched among the trees and our usual paths. Normally, she'd be racing to and fro, stopping abruptly to sniff at scents only she could detect in the undergrowth; haring off. I found her absence alarming and the woods less welcoming.

Close to tears, I made my way to the large entrance gate, thinking maybe she was waiting for me there. I was beginning to get frightened. She was Uncle Jim's dog. Mostly he was kind but he had a temper. If he got upset, there was no knowing what could happen. He always apologised afterwards, and he never hurt me, but it was scary.

I re-traced our steps. The ground was damp. Roots as big as branches protruded in places, ready to trip me if I didn't watch my footing. Under the canopy of trees, it was cold.

Along the top section of the woods, a narrow,

compacted mud path ran parallel to the backs of the houses on my street. Neighbours tipped rubbish onto it—small items mainly—dolls' prams with missing wheels, broken bicycles, teddies without heads.

Where the walls were low, I peered into the gardens but didn't stare too long for fear of invisible eyes behind blank window panes. Eyes whose owners could report back to mum.

At a certain point, heading downwards, the path turned right where the park was separated from the cemetery by a metal wire fence. It was a forbidden place, where only animals ventured, birds nested and the dead decomposed.

At the bottom of the hill the woods opened onto a vast green space sloping towards the swings and slide. Where was she? "Zoe," I called again.

Following the lower line of trees, I then took a diagonal path upwards, heading back to where I'd started.

Half-way along, a glimpse of red caught my eye.

In a small clearing I'd never noticed before, Zoe was sitting on the lap of a girl perched on a tree stump. Sunlight broke through the clouds and trees, streaming over them. Zoe had that glazed look in her eyes as she let herself be caressed and fussed over.

I was relieved and cross. "There you are. I've been looking for you everywhere." Zoe didn't run to me or show any sign of recognition but continued to let herself be stroked.

"Hello, I'm Ella. Is this your dog?" The girl was wearing a red party frock and shiny matching shoes. Mum would've said she wasn't dressed for playing and definitely not with a drooling, muddy dog.

"Yes," I said, then remembered what the priest preached on Sundays about telling the truth. "Well, no. She's like my dog, but she's actually Uncle Jim's."

"She's so pretty." Ella rubbed Zoe's ears. "And friendly. What's your name? Do you want to play?"

I was still calming down, knowing I wouldn't have to explain losing Zoe. "I can't stay for long. I have to take her back and then I have to help Mum clear up my mess."

"If you don't tell me your name, I'll make one up."

"Lisa."

Zoe moved her head from side to side as we talked. Then she jumped down, picked up a stick and dropped it at my feet. I bent and hugged her. She wriggled free and touched the stick with her wet nose. I threw it and watch her leap after it.

"Do you want to see something secret?" Ella smiled sweetly. Her skin was pale and her hair tumbled in ringlets just like in the picture books.

I hesitated.

"It'll be quick."

"Okay." When Zoe came back, I put on her lead.

"You promise not to tell?"

I nodded.

"Close your eyes."

I wasn't sure about that. I'd been told not to talk to strangers or accept sweets but no-one had said anything about girls my own age in red.

"You can trust me. Cross my heart, hope to die." She flicked her hand over her chest. Her brown eyes held mine with such intensity, I let go of any doubt. Zoe tugged at the lead.

Ella's hand was warm when it took mine. "Don't open them 'til I say."

I wanted to, just a bit, so I could see through my eyelashes, but it was also exciting, so I didn't. Mum disliked me playing with the children in our street and I was often on my own or just with Zoe or with Uncle Jim when he babysat, but he didn't count.

Ella pulled me along.

Not being able to see anything, I strained to hear. Birds fluttered and called, there were rustlings everywhere and, in the distance, the hum of the city.

I stumbled a couple of times.

"Now, open them." She finally said, when coming to a halt.

We were standing by the metal fence. On the other side, graves leaned under the weight of the overgrowth. In there—silence.

I looked around.

"I'll go first." She bent down and pulled at a loose piece of fencing where there was a shallow dip in the soil. "Hold the fence."

"I don't think we're allowed" I whispered.

"Who's going to tell?" She waved her hand in the direction of the graves and cast a furtive look behind her. "Who's going to see?"

"God," I said, a little shakily. I wanted to play with Ella but didn't want to get into trouble. "God sees everything. And he tells the priest. And the priest tells Mum."

Ella's laugh pealed into the air. "Is that what you

think?"

"Yes."

Then her face became serious. "God doesn't exist. They only tell you that so you'll do what they say. God doesn't see anything. And, if he did, how do you think he'd get to all the churches across the whole country, and the whole world even, and tell on all the children?"

I hadn't thought about that and didn't have an answer.

"Now, are you coming?" She gathered her dress and stood patiently. "Don't be a scaredy-cat."

I took a deep breath and pulled up the fence, letting her wriggle underneath.

"Now, your turn."

The ground was hard under my knees. Zoe followed, tail wagging.

Once inside, I felt the silence pulse. Trees towered, vines entwined, stones and trunks moulded together.

For a moment, I wanted to scramble back to the woods but Ella squeezed my hand.

"Come on. Follow me," she urged. We ran past fractured graves, weathered statues, a mausoleum, up-turned tombs and cracked crypts. I was surprised how quickly she moved, fearful too she'd disappear and I'd never find my way out. I was glad Zoe was with me. We tumbled against the quiet.

Suddenly, we came upon an angel.

"This is Gran," Ella said, stopping, catching her breath. Colour had risen in her cheeks. Mine were hot and I'd started to get a stitch. The tall statue poised at a strange angle had outstretched hands; its face was gentle, though the tip of the chin and one of its wings was missing.

"No, not that." She pulled me around to the side. "Look." A gaping hole dropped beneath us. Hanging over it—in the embrace of gnarled roots and vegetation—the dark wooden corner of a box peeped out.

"It's her coffin. She's asleep inside. I never met her. She was dead before I was..." Ella reached out and touched the wood.

I'd never seen a coffin.

"Do you want to lie under the magic tree?" She headed towards a large yew and crawled under its overhanging branches.

"Let's pretend we're stars," she called out.

I crept in beside her, lay on my back and spread out my arms and legs like she'd done; sensed the tips of her hands and feet at my extremities; felt an odd sensation in the pit of my stomach—part warm, part sick; dry coughed as disturbed particles in the air found their way up my nose and into my mouth.

The tree was heavy with darkness and tiny green leaves. Its branches seemed to sink towards me with each of my breaths. "I'm scared," I whispered.

"Don't be. Now, imagine yourself high in the sky, an angel looking down."

I tried to imagine seeing the earth from above. Instead, I was sinking into the ground with the roots of the tree weaving over me; suffocating, filling me with panic. I screamed but there was no sound. Then, nothing.

When I woke, my head and limbs were aching. Zoe was asleep on my chest and there was no sign of Ella. I began to cry, not knowing what had happened or how to get home.

Zoe woke up and barked. She started to sniff around, then took a direction. I grabbed the lead and she sniffed our way to the fence. We scrambled underneath and ran out of the woods, along my street to Uncle Jim's house.

He was asleep in his chair, newspaper spread over his belly. I hung Zoe's lead on its hook, changed her bowl of water, filled the dish with food, kissed her goodbye, then, closing the door quietly, hurried home.

Mum was furious. "Where have you been? Why are you covered in mud? And, why do you look so pale?

"Well, that's it, in to the bath. Naughty girl. Wait 'til your dad gets home."

She scrubbed my body 'til it gleamed and stung. I knew not to cry out. The rest of the day I was locked in my room.

That night, at the dinner table, Mum said, "I don't know what's got into her. Disappearing for hours on end with not so much as a sorry when she comes through the door and me worried out of my mind."

"Where were you?" Dad asked.

"Playing with Ella in the park, and Zoe." I knew not to say woods because I'd been told bad people waited in there for girls like me. And, I definitely knew not to say cemetery.

For a moment, Mum paled and cast a quick glance at Dad. He made a noise as if he'd been winded.

There was a pause then she snapped, "She better not be one of the girls from along the street."

Tears welled up inside me. "Zoe ran off and I thought I'd lost her but I hadn't because she found Ella and then I found both of them. I don't know where Ella lives."

After we'd eaten, Dad took me upstairs and smacked me on my bottom with the stick until I wailed.

Later, when we were sitting on the bed, he said, "You mustn't worry your mother. Do you understand?"

"Yes, Dad," I sniffed.

"Go and apologise." He handed me a tissue. "And don't sniff."

"Yes, Dad." My bottom burned and I was washed out from tears.

"And, if you meet this Ella again, don't mention her to Mum."

"Yes, Dad."

"Sorry, Mum," I said, when I got down the stairs. I wasn't really sorry in the sense that I thought I'd done anything wrong but I knew there'd be trouble if I didn't say it.

She smiled. "That's my good girl. Here, you can have some of the chocolate cake mix."

It was too sweet on my tongue but I ate it.

"What do you say?" Dad had come quietly into the room.

"Thank you, Mum."

Next time I saw Ella was a few days after I found Uncle Jim asleep on the floor and couldn't wake him.

They took him to hospital. He couldn't speak and his skin was yellow. Mum didn't really want me to go but Dad said it was important for me to see life in all its ugliness. In the days that followed, relatives I'd never seen before came to the house. They all sat in our living room talking about when Uncle Jim was a boy. Mum was busy, and cross and kept asking me to bring things in from the kitchen. I was worried about Zoe because Mum refused to have her and she was going to be taken away to stay with people she didn't know.

Ella was sitting on the bench at the top of the woods near the entrance gate. She beckoned me over with a hand holding a lit cigarette. I was pleased to see her; it was nice to have some sort of friend even if she had left me alone last time.

"Hello," she said. Her hair was shorter and loop rings hung from her ears. I wasn't allowed to pierce mine—Mum said it was common.

"Where have you been?" I asked, sitting next to her.

"Here."

"I haven't seen you."

"I'm not always sociable. Doesn't mean I don't see you." She flicked ash to the ground.

"Why did you run off last time?"

"You were asleep. I had things to do. Where's Zoe?"

Then I thought about what mum would say if she heard I was sitting on the bench with a smoking girl. "Can we go somewhere else?"

"If you want. Shall we see Gran?"

"You promise to stay with me? Zoe's not here to show me the way back."

"Cross my heart."

The angel had lost a hand and the coffin was completely hidden in ivy. Crows cawed. A humid breeze played.

Warmth enveloped us. Ella reached through the vegetation and touched the coffin.

The yew tree was covered in red berries. She picked one off, put it in her mouth then lit another cigarette.

"Do you want some?" she said, holding it out to me.

I shook my head.

"Scared or something?" She cleared a small area at the foot of the statue and began to make a small pile of berries.

"If you smoke you die."

Ella laughed and inhaled from the cigarette deeply then exhaled. "See. I'm not dead. So, where's Zoe?"

"She's had to go away until Uncle Jim gets better."

"What's wrong with him?"

"I don't know."

Ella puffed her mouth and pushed smoke rings into the air. "Well, is he ill, ill? Or just unwell?"

I thought about the visit to the hospital and Uncle Jim's body sucking in air. "Ill, ill." It made me sad. Even though he was a bit mean sometimes, I didn't want anything bad to happen to him. And, he was nice to Zoe. "Mum says he's being punished because he's a wicked sinner and that's what will happen to me if I don't do as I'm told."

Ella made herself comfortable next to the pile of berries. The sun streamed over the angel towering silently above her. "What do you think?"

"I don't know."

"You must think something."

"Uncle Jim gets bad-tempered and he can shout a lot, but he hasn't done anything like kill someone. Not as far as I know."

"Then he's not a wicked sinner."

I was relieved about this. "But what if he dies?"

"That's just life." She giggled, "well, death actually." She picked up a couple of berries and put them in her mouth.

A breeze pulled at the leaves of the trees around us. Rustling started up in the undergrowth.

"Have one." Ella seemed to glow in the rays of sun as she held out the berries on her palm.

I put one in my mouth. It tasted strange but not unpleasant. I took another.

I was dizzy and floating.
And sinking.
And suffocating.
And nothing.

When I woke, Ella was lying with her hands behind her head looking at the sky.

"You didn't leave."

She laughed. "I'll always be here."

LOUISE GETHIN

Writing about Love, Death and anything in between, Louise Gethin writes short fiction and scripts. In 2013, she self-published a collection of stories and poetic pieces with the help of fellow writer, Andy Gibb; and contributed to *Bristol Women Writers' Unchained*, an anthology celebrating the 400th anniversary of Bristol's original chained library (writersunchained.wordpress.com/anthology).

Her work has been performed at the Bristol Festival of Literature as part of the annual Redcliffe Caves event with the Bristol Writers Group.

As a child, she lived and played close to a cemetery which inspired her story Angel.

Once The Trees

GRACE PALMER

Grace Palmer

Brambles scurried over the gravestones and reclaimed their land. Martin tutted and walked on until he found a grave with an inscription he had not examined before.

Clara Englestaff. Fell asleep, aged four months. March 19th, 1889.

He looked left and right and, seeing no one in sight, pulled out the secateurs from his pocket. On top of little Clara spears of sycamore saplings hid amongst the couch grass. If they thickened they'd become trees. Once the trees set in, you could turn your back and the next thing you knew they'd be forty feet tall. In the neglected areas of the cemetery their long upright trunks created dense woodland, wrecking graves and upending masonry. The secateurs struggled as he chopped the sapling stems off below each brown bud. They sheared through the stems with a satisfying crunch.

Poppy pulled on her lead. She was good company on his daily walk around Arnos Vale Cemetery. He remembered the squally spring day when they'd rescued her, a sad little puppy sitting in a cage, that stank of fear and Jeyes Fluid, at the Dogs Home. It was early on in their relationship when Cathy had persuaded him they needed a dog. He told her he didn't want any extra disruption.

"It's heart-breaking," she'd said looking at Poppy. Then she rubbed her thumb over the delicate skin of his palm, shooting lust, love and tenderness through his body and so he'd said yes, on the understanding that Cathy looked after her. He'd been surprised how much he enjoyed the dog, who trotted by his side on their country walks to Wellow, Coombe Dingle and Butcombe, returning sticks he threw, wagging her tail.

Later, they'd sit either side of the wood-burner, Poppy between them on the rug. To break the tight silence he'd talk about the dog, or he'd murmur, "Good girl, Good girl," to the loyal terrier. He had tried to teach Cathy. How to load the dishwasher, how he liked his pasta firm and not a heap of wet slime. How he hated Radio Two in the morning and needed silence on his return from work. He had tried.

Now Cathy was gone he wouldn't be without Poppy. Faithful Poppy never roamed in search of love. She lived to please and rubbed her nose into his curled hand and looked up with limpid eyes. When he called, she'd come, when he told her off, she'd lower her head. Good Dog. He scratched her favourite spot behind her collar. The wind whipped, rain misted the air and the dog shivered. He needed a coffee and deserved a cherry flapjack. Another twenty minutes and he'd be sitting in the Spielman Cafe in the old Crypt at the bottom of the cemetery. On a day like this there shouldn't be too many kids. And, if there were, he could talk to Poppy.

With the rain thickening his horizon narrowed. He set off, glad of his boots as the path turned muddier. He'd take the short cut through the oldest part of the graveyard. He opened the ornate iron gate, set into a ramshackle fence patched with wooden pointed staves. This part of the cemetery had been sectioned off, perhaps by some ancient Victorian family to show they were above the riff raff. Sure enough, the monuments were grandiose. He stopped before a huge bath tub on legs, spouting complicated family relationships set in stone, commemorating the dead. Another dead baby Clara. 1852. This was most unusual; two Claras in one day. He noted the names of those who'd died in his pocket book. He thought of the other C. It had never bothered him once the smell had gone, and everything was clean again, but it meant he couldn't sell the house.

On he walked past Celtic crosses, obelisks and angels guarding burial sites. Trees grew straight and close, extinguishing light at ground level. Roots crowbarred graves open and crushed leaves spread a mix of spores and fungi into the air. He fingered his secateurs in his pocket. It was too late for those. The groundsmen were clearly not up to the job of looking after this cemetery. Tomorrow he'd bring a saw and set to work, let a little light into the grounds. Order needed to be restored. Everything in its rightful place. Untidiness, decay, fungi and disease would be eradicated. He wasn't an unreasonable man, but things needed to be dealt with before the trees took over and this became a wood.

Through the foliage he caught a glimpse of a black,

three-wheeled buggy. Mothers, out on a day like this. They ought to be tucked up with their infants, safe and warm, in front of a crackling log-burner, chilli in the oven, waiting for their better halves.

The path curved, and tree roots popped like knuckles from the mud. He trod carefully but still slipped on the black path. He grabbed a branch, slid onto his backside and yanked his shoulder. The branch bent with his weight and the tree creaked. He looked up at a toppling vision, a circle of thin tree trunks reaching for the light like children's hands. Pain throbbed through his shoulder, the branch would not hold him, he had to let go. He fell, banged his back against the path, bumped his head on a stone, his body carrying him down the mud-slide before he came to a stop, winded. Bile rose in his throat, hot and green. Poppy yelped and he lost the lead. The bitch had run away, deserted him too. He'd punish her later, show her who was boss.

Now the rain clouded the air like the veils cast across stone angel's faces. He touched his head and his hand came away decorated with green tree muck and blood. Water dripped down his neck. He wiped his trousers in disgust and watched the rain needling his jacket. He stood up, gingerly, and walked on through the wild vegetation, his head pinched and aching. If he could get to the cafe, away from the smothering ivy and the keening wind, away from graves broken like biscuits, gaping with air where soil should have been, then he'd feel better. The rain stung his face and his kidneys ached where he'd fallen.

There was something in the air like an electrical

current, perhaps there'd be lightning. A blackbird chinked, and a baby cried. Normal noises. He caught a glimpse of the black buggy again through the trees.

The rain hissed and beyond that the baby's cries grew louder. The cry was plaintive, the sort building up to hysteria, a sound demanding attention. Surely the woman could stop the racket?

A fleeting glance of Poppy in the distance, not even looking shame-faced. Bitch. Deserter.

He wanted the tamp of the cafe's barista, the selection of cakes, he wanted the fug of the cafe. He needed to reach the area where the trees had been controlled. This short cut seemed interminable, leading him past ivy turned to rock-stone and tree roots feeding into the spaces above the coffins. It was mistake to bury people on slopes. Animals could get in and gravity could do its dirty work, distending the soil. Far better to bury corpses on flat ground.

The rain beat so hard that he could easily lose his footing again. He sheltered under a tree growing out of a grave to wait out the worst of it. He had no qualms about standing above a coffin, superstitions were for fools. The tree yielded to his back, like a wooden futon. He whistled for Poppy. She ran towards him then whimpered and wouldn't come closer. A definite thrashing for her. Everyone betrayed him in the end. But there were consequences and people got what they deserved.

The cries of the baby seemed nearer, the noise a needle-pain inside his throbbing head. He glanced back. The woman with the buggy was behind him, coming down the path. Silly cow. Her head was hidden behind a fake fur parka, a cheap coat for a woman with an expensive buggy.

The baby's cries were jagged now, rising with hysteria. Some people. She ought to be at home, not pushing a baby in a storm. Well he wasn't going to help her navigate the path. The mud squelched as the buggy's wheels pushed through. He examined the eyelets on his boots, so he wouldn't have to see the woman. Poppy whined, barked sharply once, twice, then ran away, as fast as if he'd thrown a ball.

The woman's breath was ragged, and the baby worked itself up into a rage. She was getting nearer. He kicked at the tree to get rid of the mud on his boots, so he could continue his walk after the woman had gone. The buggy stopped parallel to him, he could see the glinting wheels. Outraged by the impertinence he looked up. Cathy stared from inside the faux fur parka and smiled the same smile she'd worn when she'd told him she was leaving, before he'd fixed her, and she'd disappeared under the polished boards.

The flesh on her face dropped like wax and a pitted skull emerged, dripping grey matter. A skeletal arm stretched toward him. He recoiled but the tree held him steady and one bone-finger pressed deep into his chest. He could not move, her eye sockets held him fast. Then the thing that was Cathy gestured for him to look inside the buggy.

A mess of half limbs in a sac; a jellied comma.

"You were pregnant?"

The thing nodded.

"You two-timing slut."

"It's yours," she cried.

Poppy howled in the distance.

Behind him the sycamore drew him tight into its trunk.

Behind him the trees signalled through roots and fungi networks.

Behind him the trees reached to the sky like children.

GRACE PALMER

Grace Palmer is self-employed as a Creative Writing tutor and director of Novel Nights, creating live lit events for writers in Bristol and Bath. Growing up as the fifth child in a family of six on a farm in the middle of nowhere created ideal conditions for becoming a writer - solitude and the fact everyone was too busy to listen. Since she completed an MA in Creative Writing at Bath Spa University her stories have been published in *FlashBack Fiction, Flash Fiction One & Two, & Riggwelter Press* (2019).

Over the years she's been invited to read at Bath and Bristol literature festivals and slams. Her favourite near-miss is being longlisted for the Bristol Short Story Prize.

She plans to conquer her fear of heights by asking her rock-climbing son to teach her to abseil.

Darkfall

Dev Agarwal

Petra watched the old woman limp into the camp with the latest roundup of new arrivals. The chargehands led her group onto the scrap land in front of the barracks block and the bleeding posts. Petra peeked while she worked—that was safe enough as the owners weren't nearby.

This roundup was small, just ten men and women. Petra sensed that the owners planned something. It was in the air—they were tense, more alert. They'd even killed a chargehand that morning. Slasher had done it, losing his temper when the hand fumbled the bread ration.

The ten new workers, probably taken from around Bristol, stood in a row. Petra understood their confusion. She remembered stumbling through the city, swept up in the turmoil of the darkfall at the start of the collapse.

When the owners caught her, Petra had been rigid with terror. The owners, hissing and screeching, ordered her group of survivors to follow them. Petra and the others were led to a camp in a wasteland of rubble. The only structures still standing were the two houses that the owners and chargehands each used, the barrack blocks and the six-foot posts. All other buildings nearby had been demolished.

Petra later worked to clear more of the land by hand. It was hard now to see how big the wasteland was that they'd created or where the neighbourhoods of Bristol lay.

Everything was indistinct in the permanent twilight of the darkfall. Today a light mist, dirty with grit permeated the poor atmosphere.

The new captives stood still, nearly catatonic at being this close to the owners. The chargehands stripped them naked and threw shifts and scraps of underwear to each of them. For those foolish enough to start dressing, the top chargehand, ugly Delmar, slapped their heads with a whip made out of a heavy plastic cable.

A tall figure stepped out of the owners' house. The Ogre. He towered over the workers, his skin was starkly white in his red robes, and his limbs looked too long for his body. He picked through the group by flicking his fingers at each captive's shoulders. His fingers barely made contact but each man or woman reeled at his touch. Petra knew that sensation. She'd been singled out herself by an owner before, then taken and tied to a post and bled. She'd been lucky in the week that she'd been in the camp. It had only happened to her once, and she hadn't been bled to death.

Petra watched the group. But she gave them only the barest of glances now that the Ogre had appeared, while she dragged rubble behind the barrack block. The Ogre had chosen the old woman. The woman looked sixty, but was probably a lot younger—the collapse and the darkfall had been tough on everyone. Her hair was streaked heavily with grey, and her reddened eyes blinked continuously in the gritty mist. *Someone's grandmother*, Petra thought.

The woman swayed, looking exhausted, but she made it into the huddle of workers.

Good for you, Petra thought. Four people from the roundup remained behind. Hunched over, with one coughing and another crying uncontrollably. They were cast-offs, too sick or weak to work. The chargehands would beat them to death, or the owners would take them to the posts and feed.

The old woman kept looking round, trying to concentrate, drinking in information now she was a captive.

She'd need to be more careful, Petra knew. Acting too alert or with too much eye contact meant punishment.

They herded the naked prisoners past Petra, each clutching their bundles of unwashed shifts. When the woman stumbled, Petra reached out and steadied her; surprising herself.

"Thank you," the woman said. She hesitated, then said, "I'm Anna—"

"No talking," Petra said. The owners allowed only the most basic instructions between workers. Even chargehands barely spoke.

It was only much later, lying on straw in the barracks, pressed too close by the crowded bodies to stretch out fully, that they talked—they kept their voices low.

"Our owners are the strigoi," Petra said. "It's the old

name for vampire."

The woman, Anna, said, "A week of this and I can still barely believe this has happened. This darkness."

"Many workers could not. They died first," Petra said.

"These men, they are barbaric."

"The strigoi are not men. They're monsters."

"What happens in this camp? Why are we here?" Anna asked.

"You work twelve hours. Clearing rubble, tearing down buildings, or digging ditches. Those too weak are taken by the owners. The owners drink, or if they're bored or angry, they *eat*."

"They eat us?" Anna whispered.

"They have always done so. They've always been there, but hidden. We just didn't know the strigoi were out there."

"And they caused the darkfall?"

Petra nodded. "That's what it looks like. With the sky permanently dark they walk among us out in the open."

"How long have you been in this camp?"

"A week. Since the collapse and the day of the darkfall. I was looking for food—mostly from houses people had abandoned. I didn't know why people were missing. I thought they had fled Bristol. Then I saw the strigoi and their chargehands. I knew to keep well away." Petra almost laughed. If you grew up running from the police, you learned how to run from chargehands and strigoi.

"Dear God, you poor child."

Petra thought about how she might answer that. Before the camp, before the darkfall, she had been a girl. Seventeen and newly free of her care home—if not free of the scars of Children's Services and her chain of broken foster families. Scars that were laughable now. Petra remembered the first moment of the darkfall. How the midday sun vanished, swept under the ink stain that spread across the summer sky above Bristol. In a vortex of screaming, of cars crashing across Temple Way and birds scattered and panicking in the abruptly dark sky, Petra had started running.

But rather than attempting to say any of that, Petra said, "Sleep. Save your strength. Tomorrow they'll work us again."

Anna nodded. "Yes, let's sleep. But remember child, there has to be something worth saving our strength for."

Vic Edmond's foraging led him to Arnos Vale. He had forgotten about the cemetery. Forgotten everything when the dark sky turned his world upside down. Now, coming across it by accident, Vic made a snap decision. He walked along the perimeter wall, looking for a way in. The cemetery might be remote enough that no one would look inside. No shops inside the graveyard, but the Spielman Centre possibly had food left over. Giving up on the locked gate, Vic ran forward and scrambled over the wall. At six foot two he grasped the top comfortably. The bricks were wet from the heavy mist.

Vic dropped inside, next to lines of cedars and pines. Stepping through the tall trees led him to a path, curving in a loop round a garden of rest. Ahead of him, visible in the twilight stood the Spielman Centre. He recognised the four tall Roman columns of its façade.

Vic stalked along the path, trying to sense trouble. He snorted at himself. He was a fund manager, what did he know about sensing anything? Tall buildings rose out of the mist, hard to see, but still solid wedges of concrete among the greenery. Past them he knew were graves and tombstones. Mossy-backed, run down, or bright and new. There were waves of them as the cemetery grew with new dead. Now Bristol was littered with corpses all lying unburied.

He reached the steps of the Spielman Centre before he knew anyone was waiting.

"Stop right there," a voice said, pitched low, but carrying in the stillness of the mist and darkness.

Vic hesitated, caught between obeying and running.

A stocky figure in a leather jacket stepped out of the glass doors of the centre.

"What are you doing here?" He had an American accent. Southern too, almost drawling.

The man was heavy in the shoulders and looked a hard fifty years old, gnarled like a fighter.

"Who are you?" Vic asked.

"Johnny Monrose," the American said. Vic was so surprised to get an answer that it silenced him. Monrose didn't offer to shake hands, but he did say, "What's your name?"

"Vic Edmond."

Monrose said, "So what are you doing here?"

Vic didn't like answering to this stranger, but he said, "Well I was hiding in a loft with my son and my wife. A gang kicked in the front door and looted our kitchen. I just had it put in." He laughed nervously at himself.

"Your family still alive?"

Vic nodded. "And they're hungry. There's no food there. There's no food in any shop for miles around. I've trekked here from Keynsham."

"Keynsham. That a nice part of town?" Monrose asked. Perhaps he'd noticed Vic's suit, or the shine of his Tag Heuer on his wrist.

"Yes, fairly nice. I've got to find food for them."

"Be thankful they're still alive," Monrose said.

"I do, thank God."

Monrose glanced round. "So how'd you know the graveyard would be safe?"

"You mean with those things out there?"

"Yeah. *Those things.* The strigoi."

"I know that some of the ground is consecrated in here."

"Good thinking," Monrose said. He glanced round. "This is an old place, right?"

Vic nodded. "Victorian. Lot of famous men of science got buried here. And a lot of old rich bankers too."

"You one of those guys? Businessman too?"

Vic said, "I was. Fund manager. Then this happened."

Monrose nodded. "Darkfall."

Vic said, "And with the sunlight gone, monsters have come out."

"Or the other way round." Monrose stepped closer. "Those strigoi out there? They've always been there. But now they've made the sky dark an' they're right where everyone can see them. They don't care. They're scared of the sun. It's kept them in place for long years.

Millennia. But without it they're dominant again."

"Again?"

He nodded. "They're as old as humanity. They walked the earth before. Out in the open, like they are now. They shared the land with us. Right at the dawn of man."

Monrose spoke with a slow, methodical tone. Sounding like he knew what he spoke of.

"The strigoi bred humans once. We were their cattle— their food. We came out of Africa together, two species, coexisting. There were always fewer of them than us," Monrose said. "Someone worked out how to fight them. The old ways work best. The strigoi fear fire most of all—and the sun, of course."

"How do you know this?" Vic asked.

"I was part of a group. We hunted the strigoi. My bossman is with us." He flicked his head back a bare inch, across to the gardens of rest and into the consecrated ground. "Major Sinclair."

"You're in the army?"

"We were. Special unit. The strigoi was the ultimate covert war."

Vic easily believed that this tough-talking American was some kind of soldier. But if so, that was in the life before darkfall. Before the strigoi rose up out of the shadows.

"How'd that happen? The darkfall?"

Monrose shook his head. "That shit took us by surprise. They did something. They're not human. Who knows what they can do? There are fewer of them than humanity—but each one is a lot stronger. They're tough to kill and very long-lived."

"Do you know what they want?" Vic asked.

Monrose nodded. "That part's simple. They want to win."

Two hundred workers were trapped in the camp, digging the earth bare-handed or dragging bricks and masonry as the buildings were broken down and cleared. Petra worked alongside Anna now. She was surprised at how much strength she could draw from this new, immediate friendship. Working all day became easier, more possible, despite the bare rations of bread and soup.

There was just one more day of that before the owners broke the routine again.

The head chargehand, Delmar, shouted at the workers to line up. Delmar was angry. But he was *always* angry. Enraged at being a chargehand or at the man or owner that had scarred his face. One ear was a stub, the flesh pink and ugly into the burned and mottled stubble of his shaved head. His rage kept him at the top of the camp hierarchy.

The workers fell into position and the strigoi circled their ranks. Swollen with power, they were immaculate in their clean robes. Slender, perfumed, they strode like gods. Violence amused them. This role-reversal amused them. They were the winners now. They had defeated humanity.

To Petra's surprise, the strigoi ordered the chargehands to lead them out of the camp. Delmar gave the other hands orders and they herded the workers into the city's streets. All two hundred of them were marched, in columns, their heads bent before their owners.

The workers' footsteps echoed in their ragged line, first across the river and then through Bedminster and Victoria Park. The mist settled in a white coverlet over the silent city as they were led down Redcatch Road. It turned the buildings into bulbous shapes, their facades melting as the workers trudged past.

Walking beside Anna, Petra grew dizzy with hunger and her feet hurt in her thin shoes.

But Petra had also made herself strong. Not physically, but inside, where it counted. She taught herself how to survive since she first went into care. Petra even chose her own name. She rejected her birth name, Emily. She buried it. Emily had been a baby, helpless when her dad walked away and her family descended into the chaos of her mum's alcoholism and each new boyfriend, more disturbed than the last.

Petra was born in the foster placements that always broke down or the children's homes of Belluton and Winford.

Petra survived each of them and she would survive *this* world too. She stopped thinking. She liked avoiding thinking. It was a special state of being. Not thinking and not caring. She would not give the owners the satisfaction of her fear. Instead, she followed the strigoi as they marched with purpose. The workers tramped down empty streets. Later, they slowed to weave between abandoned cars. Squeezing between them, Petra's hands grew wet where the metal was slick with vapour from the mist.

It felt like the strigoi were marching them towards a

specific destination. Petra surprised herself. She thought she did not care, but she found hatred kindling inside her. It had lain within her, buried deep. Emotions meant risk in the camp. They meant loss of control and an owner would kill you for that quick enough. But Petra let her anger awaken, siphoning just a little out. Her rage began to warm her. Anger at the owners, at the chargehands who betrayed humanity for comforts and safety, and at the darkfall that had swallowed everything.

She carried on marching, still obeying, still working for the owners. But Petra knew that she was going to fight them. Fight them, or die trying.

Vic braced his palms against the cemetery wall. The darkfall hid his enemies from him. He was used to Bristol's looters after the gangs that had trashed his home. They barely concerned him now that he'd seen the strigoi. Monsters that looked like men. They lay in wait beyond Arnos Vale's stone walls.

He couldn't stay here. Stan and Michelle were still in Keynsham, still hiding in the loft. Vic should be with them.

Tears of frustration pricked his eyes. Monrose had convinced him to stay overnight, when the darkfall was strongest and the sky was totally blackened. At night, the darkfall was so dense it might be a black hole. One that had grown bloated and stretched over the whole sky. Vic marvelled at how nothing escaped it. Not the sun, nor the moon, not the smallest glint of the stars shone any more. It took the full light of noon for the sky to brighten at all. Then a little light broke through.

But Vic couldn't stand it any longer. Being safe wasn't enough. Since he'd been here, he'd walked among the group of people that huddled in the cemetery. They were hunched and listless among the mass of Victorian mausoleums and tombstones. They'd gathered here by religious belief or dumb luck. Survivors, not fighters. They'd welcomed him, shared their food with him. That had helped a lot. Vic felt more alert now, better able to concentrate.

Fortified, restless, he'd walked behind the old Anglican chapel and up to the graveyard's main wall. It rose six feet, almost his height. Beyond it lay the main road, the shadows of infrequent old trees, oaks and ash, and abandoned cars. Mist streamed through them, a milky river that ran back to the town. And over everything, hung the oppressive weight of the sky.

On tiptoe, Vic reached up to the top of the wall. He pressed wet moss that he couldn't see against the brickwork. Time to go.

"You leaving us, Mr Edmond?"

Startled, Vic stepped back and turned quickly.

Monrose's friend, Sinclair, stood waiting for him. He was almost hidden among the shadows cast by the chapel behind them.

Sinclair stood relaxed, with his weight leaning leftwards, almost as if balanced where the ground undulated. For a moment, Vic imagined that they stood alone in a dark, rolling sea. The white caps of gravestones formed the tops of waves cresting over them both.

"I have to go," Vic said. "My son. He's out there."

Vic had not spoken to Sinclair yet. Monrose told him Sinclair was injured and he'd been sleeping when Vic arrived. But Vic knew who he was—Monrose's only ally inside the graveyard.

Sinclair smiled and shook his head. His hair was a startling white. "You're free to go, but I'd advise against it. You can't help him. Not that way."

"I can't leave them there," Vic said. But to his shame, fear rushed him, turning his knees weak. He could imagine hiding out here, safe enough on sacred ground.

"Getting killed isn't helping anyone. Stay put, here with us."

Vic leaned against the wall. The moment for climbing it had passed, for now. Sinclair turned and Vic fell into step with him. They walked back to where the other survivors waited. There were about twenty-five of them, all white people—but Vic was used to being the only black man in a crowd. Deeper into the graveyard stood a stone obelisk, carved as a memorial years ago. Behind stood another, smaller, as if a receding mirror image. But he knew both had been built long ago by proud Victorians.

Monrose had found these civilians inside the cemetery, using the Spielman Centre for shelter. Under Sinclair's directions, he'd moved them, brought them to wait in the open among the graves beside the Anglican chapel. Less cover from the elements, but better, on consecrated ground.

"I know you spoke to Johnny. He told you about our unit?"

Vic nodded.

"We were called Mockingbird. And we were winning." Sinclair said. "We pushed the strigoi down till all anyone remembered were folk tales and scare stories. Now look where we are." He almost laughed. "They're stronger than ever. They created the darkfall. Beyond the River Avon they're rounding up people as slave labour, starving them down to sticks and clearing the land by hand. All fire is banned. That's the future they promise us. Humanity bred as cattle."

Vic was about to reply when a tall figure loomed out of the shadows of the Anglican chapel and said to Sinclair, "Come here, you fucking cripple." Almost an afterthought, the man punched Vic hard in the face. Vic slammed into a grave stone, his eyesight white with starbursts of light.

Staring upwards, through tears and retinal flares, Vic saw the tall man pounce on Sinclair. The man's head was covered in an old burn, one ear pink and torn into a stub. He looked unstoppable, but Vic found himself climbing back up, dragging his body forward and lunging after them as Sinclair shrank from the attack.

Vic heard shouting behind them from the crowd. He collided into the man's long legs in a sideways barge. Like hitting a brick wall. The man kicked backwards and Vic spun away, his shoulder on fire where a heel dug into his muscle.

An ear-splitting explosion ripped over Vic's head. Above him, the tall man's face turned white and his mouth formed a silent O of amazement. He stepped a pace backwards but then he straightened and rallied. Sinclair stood waiting. He steadied himself, still waiting.

He held a large pistol in both hands. The tall man stepped forward, wobbled and sprawled gracelessly between the gravestones.

Sinclair straightened. He pressed his forearm to his left side, as if protecting a deep injury.

Around them, the other survivors backed away, their faces wide with shock.

They thought they were safe inside the graveyard, Vic thought. So did I...

Unsteadily, he climbed to his feet.

"Sinclair. You good?"

Monrose rushed up to them. He scanned the pathways and the shadowed trees for more attackers.

"Bastard took me by surprise."

Both men seemed relaxed.

At their feet, the dead man's face remained fixed, twisted in pain. His head was lopsided, the hair missing through scar tissue, and one side of his face looked like it had turned to hot wax with its burns.

Vic blinked tears from being punched so hard.

"Is that a strigoi?" he asked.

"Traitor," Monrose said. "Just as well. Bullets don't stop strigoi."

"He's a traitor?" Vic asked.

"Sadly that's so," Sinclair said. He lowered his pistol. It was a huge revolver, silver steel, the wheel of the cylinder glinted with the blunt tips of bullets.

Sinclair said, "The strigoi use them. People who value their own life over their own kind."

Monrose said, "Consecrated ground. The strigoi can't stand to walk on it."

"So they use traitors," Sinclair said, "Men. Or humans, at least. They sided with the strigoi. Now they help turn us into slaves. And food stock."

"We're still not safe?" Vic said. He lowered his voice to avoid a panic in the crowd.

Sinclair started to laugh, till coughing overtook him. When it stopped, he spat. "There's only one kind of safety in this darkfall."

"Only one kind that there's ever been, right Major?" Monrose said, speaking with easy familiarity.

Vic's head beat with pain and his cheek felt swollen and huge. He wanted to scream. The pressure built over him, crushing his senses until he felt he was trapped inside his own head. Death, fear, his wife and son. It was all too much. Yet these two men joked as a man's corpse bled out beside them.

"The strigoi are missing a dinner," Monrose said, glancing at the dead man.

"You seem pretty relaxed," Vic said to them, tension sharpening his tone. "Considering they just tried to kill you."

"Him?" Sinclair said. "He wasn't sent to kill me."

"That guy came to take Sinclair back over the wall. Snatch squad," Monrose said.

"We are not just food to the strigoi. They're primitive in many ways, animalistic. They invest their enemies with power."

"Sinclair here is big medicine to them," Monrose said, "He fought the strigoi for thirty years. He's just about their top enemy on the planet."

"They get hold of me," Sinclair said, "they'll have lots

of fun."

Vic sensed that this gallows talk was how they had lived with their war against the strigoi for so long.

Vic looked out into the darkness. His eyes played tricks but he thought he saw something flicker through the trees again. Something pale, the body elongated and limbs spidery.

He shivered, feeling enemies close by, pressing in at him.

"You want to do something? For your family?" Sinclair asked.

Vic nodded.

"Come help us." Monrose extended his hand to Vic in comradeship. "We got plenty to do—now we know they're comin'."

The owners raced ahead of the march, speeding through the darkness. They called to each other with violin shrieks as they hunted in packs.

Slasher, the Ogre, Beauty.

Petra had told Anna her names for the owners—her act of resistance.

The owners returned to the march, sometimes empty handed, sometimes with new workers.

"More survivors from the city," Anna told her, her voice a whisper.

Anna glanced at one man, better fed than the workers—as he'd not been on their starvation rations. "He says they caught him in Queen's Square. The owners are spreading out, searching for something."

"What?"

Anna watched the chargehands—taking her moment to speak. "Something the owners want. Something important."

Petra didn't nod. She didn't do anything that an alert chargehand might see. This wasn't just chatter. Anna and Petra were scavenging, gathering scraps about the owners and their world.

Neither of them had discussed escape. The ground beyond the camp had been as blasted and empty as the moon. Stripped and broken down by waves of workers toiling in twelve-hour shifts, there was nowhere to hide, no cover to run to.

This march was the first time that Petra had left the camp. That made it an opportunity.

After a life of broken homes, and family breakdowns, Petra knew how strong and precious any opportunity was.

A worker came by, his face mottled from old beatings. He handed them a slice of stale white bread each.

Petra and Anna sat together, eating their bread with tiny bites, letting each piece do the work of a feast as their guts ground with hunger.

"You noticed?" Anna asked.

Again Petra didn't nod, but she said, "Delmar. Where is he?"

"That's right. He went out hours ago."

Glancing round at the crowd of workers, Anna said, "It's like a medieval army. The owners have brought everyone with them. Not just themselves and the chargehands. We're all here, a train of slaves and camp followers."

Petra didn't understand what all those words meant.

Anna said, "They don't plan to return to their camp."

The food break ended and the chargehands hurried the workers further into the silent town. The pace grew too fast, too urgent for everyone. Workers struggled and then fell out of place. The chargehands descended on the stragglers. They beat them and left the bodies bloody-faced and abandoned where they fell.

Marching, feeling the tarmac vibrate through her feet, Petra fought to concentrate. Once she'd fought to lose herself, to mentally escape her life as a worker. Now fear and anger warred inside her and she pushed those feelings back. Being with Anna gave her strength.

Resist, Petra told herself.

Anna had said once, "Remember the old world, so you keep a piece of it alive inside you." Petra did that now, fighting to hold onto herself even as the owners took everything else.

Arnos Vale rang with activity. Monrose had roused the men and women huddled among the gravestones and sent them running with jobs. Vic scuttled to the main gate and back, carrying furniture back to the chapel. Monrose unlocked the gates and led gangs of people, working in chains. Everyone had been nervous at leaving the cemetery and stepping off from consecrated ground.

"We all do just a little," Monrose said, and led them by example. They went in small groups across the silent

Bath Road, looting, scratching together resources. Or Monrose sent people into the Spielman Centre or the West Lodge at the front gate. They rushed back to Sinclair, carrying furniture, curtains, anything that Monrose selected for use.

Behind the chapel, Major Sinclair directed people to stack their salvage at the edges of the consecrated ground. He had to lean against a gravestone, his old injury leaving him breathless. Sinclair still carried his hefty pistol, but Monrose always had someone stationed with him. Around them, people worked, active and purposeful. They were not just surviving now, they were challenging the strigoi.

Monrose's scavengers brought back loads of wood, tables, chairs, even sideboards. Sinclair organised bundles of wood, laying out lumpen channels across pathways. If these were barricades, they would be easy to cross between or climb over. But Vic didn't question the work.

Just walking to the heavy gates of Arnos Vale, even remaining *inside* them, made Vic nauseous with fear. Small sounds turned him dizzy with adrenaline. Whenever he heard anything outside of the small tight circle of consecrated ground, he'd almost lose control.

He thought he saw a figure swaying in the trees beyond the Matthews' family memorial. The next he knew, Vic found himself crouching by an ivy laden gravestone, his own voice just below a whisper, saying "I'm not ready for this, I'm not ready for this."

It felt like a gorilla had sunk onto his back, sending him down to his knees, gasping beneath its bulk.

But Vic also found that he could recover. He climbed back to his feet and took up the next load of wood panels or old ladders and carried them back to the edge of the garden of rest to stack like a breakwater.

When the last group came in, Monrose padlocked a heavy chain across the gates and walked towards Vic.

"So what's your plan?" Vic asked. "This doesn't look like an escape."

Monrose's stare rested lightly on Vic. When he didn't reply, Vic pressed him. "You didn't come here to hide."

Monrose said, "I don't want to escape Arnos Vale, not when we spent so much time getting ready right here."

"They're coming?" Vic fought to keep his voice firm.

"They will. Soon enough." Monrose nodded. "We got something they want. But don't worry, strigoi can't touch consecrated ground."

"That's safe?" Vic thought of the man who'd attacked Sinclair.

Monrose shook his head. "No such thing. But maybe *safer*."

He set two bottles of Jim Beam down on the grass. Instead of caps, each one bore wicks, flaps of line wedged into the open neck. Vic had heard of Molotov cocktails before, but never seen them. Fund managers didn't move in those circles.

"Two firebombs and a pistol. Is that your arsenal?" he asked Monrose.

"Not too much, is it?" Monrose said. "It'll take more'n that to stop strigoi."

But Monrose seemed confident.

Vic glanced back at Sinclair.

"He's what they want?" Vic asked.

Monrose nodded. "Big medicine. Strigoi are primitive fucking animals. Back in the day, they messed Sinclair up pretty bad. An' they're still scared of him. Now they think it's their chance." Monrose was oddly toneless when he said that. Perhaps he accepted Sinclair's injuries as part of the price of war.

Monrose nodded to the men and women gathered around the chapel. They were from every walk of life. People in suits, students and the homeless. They stared around them, nervous and wired, too scared to sleep. Vic knew the gouging fear that twisted through them.

"You see them?" Monrose said. "They're good people. Workers. But not fighters. We need fighters."

And with that, Monrose jogged away, past the chapel, then each of the gardens of rest and back to the main gate.

The road passed beneath Petra's feet, uneven, potholed, edged with weeds. She kept pace with Anna. Petra had decent enough shoes; some workers walked barefoot. She had the same grey shift that the others wore and rags of underwear. Tucked under the shift she also had six inches of plastic pipe, sharpened at one end. It was the best she could do for a weapon. She and Anna had taken turns filing it down to a point and then carrying it between them.

She heard the hands talking. Barking orders, but also whispering, concerned about something. Delmar. He was missing. The hands seemed to know where he'd gone. The owners had sent him ahead and the other chargehands thought he'd failed.

"They'll kill him for it," one said. And Petra knew that was true. To the strigoi all of them, the hands included, were just meat that talked.

A chargehand called a halt and Petra's line stumbled and stopped at a knot of trees and a moss-stained wall. It looked familiar to her. The branches were sturdy and black.

The Ogre, not walking, but *gliding*, moved past them. His movements were fluid as a racehorse. A chargehand shouted, his voice hoarse, ordering the workers to step aside for the Ogre. Smiling, teeth white and even, the Ogre brushed Petra before she could step away. The barest flicker of contact on her arm but it was like an electric pulse, firing the nerve endings in her flesh.

The Ogre didn't notice her reaction and didn't care. He was already gone.

In his wake, Petra struggled to find her balance as her emotions churned within her. Just the strigoi's touch had such power.

The Ogre's head turned, canted upwards as if smelling the air. His smile widened.

Anna made the smallest noise. Petra's heart hammered. The chargehands would be watching, ready with their whips to punish a worker for the smallest noise. But they had turned too.

Petra thought she saw horses. Horses stepping out of the whiteness of the mist. Two of the things trotted forward and grew larger. They were tall as horses but hairless. Their skin was rough and ashen, either sweating or damp from the fog. Their scent was thick and musty, like wet dogs. Heavy with fat and muscle, they padded along on flat forearms and squat rear legs.

Horrified, Petra saw that they were deformed men swollen to huge size. Their bodies had been twisted into beasts. They approached, tongues lolling from their broad faces. Each beast bore a rider.

The Ogre bowed to the riders. Both were owners. One leaned down from the top of his beast. It was Beauty.

Anna had named him Beauty for his ugliness. Crooked backed, and with hair blindingly white, he was unlike the other owners. Not just old, but visibly so.

The owners spoke. The tone, if not their words carried over the still air. The beast Beauty rode shifted. Its head looked like a demented man's, with short runtish hair, an empty stare and gaping lips that drooled over its chin.

The owners had twisted humanity, reshaping it as their conquest spread. They didn't just own workers now, they made them into beasts of burden.

A noise arose from the workers. A lowing without words—a group moan of fear and disgust. The chargehands were not immune to it. One even dropped his whip.

The Ogre looked back and laughed at his slaves. His eyes shone with amusement.

Petra fought to breathe, to stay upright. She wanted to curl away and escape into memory. Then the workers were moving again, led now by Beauty and the other mounted strigoi. Petra walked forward, sickened, yet obedient. She was also acutely aware of the plastic pipe, sharpened on one end and digging into her belly.

Its time was nearing.

The sky brightened slightly. Daytime, Petra thought. Those brief hours where even the darkfall was not quite so black and overwhelming.

The workers marched across a wide road. It lay empty except for abandoned cars.

Arnos Vale. Petra recognised the cemetery now from the world before darkfall. She had come here with her friends late at night, daring each other to run among the stones.

Beauty reined his beast to a stop and leaned over to speak to the Ogre. The Ogre nodded and raised a hand to the other strigoi. Then he turned and pointed right at Anna. A chargehand strode over to her and dragged her off her feet. The chargehand ran her up to Beauty on his mount. Anna was carried so quickly she couldn't keep her balance and flailed her arms as he dragged her.

Laughing, Beauty leaned down to Anna. He reached forward with his long hands. His fingers were bent and swollen with countless decades of use but they moved with speed and force. Anna screamed as Beauty stripped the skin off her living body. He tore Anna open like she was a leaky sack. Her blood spattered his face as he tore into her soft throat and killed her.

Petra choked off the scream in her throat. Inside, she deadened herself. She felt her face turn to bone, hiding her reactions. The other workers around her did the same. The only movements were involuntary as their bodies shivered.

Petra's head pounded with the noise of Anna's death. Then in the abrupt silence as Anna's body grew slack in Beauty's grip, her scream echoed through Petra's mind. Petra shook like a terrified animal. This was what the owner's reduced her to.

I can survive this, she told herself. She squeezed her eyes shut. Just for a moment. Just for an instant of peace that no chargehand would notice.

Petra sank into the locked strong room in her mind that she had gone to as a child. She rallied there, gathering her strength to face the strigoi again. When she opened her eyes she had steeled her mind again.

Learn from it. She imagined Anna saying that to her. Her voice firm with purpose.

But all Petra had learned was that her friend was dead and the lesson was *chance*, and how random and precious life could be.

In her fear and misery, Petra was surprised by the heat burning her face. And how much better her own anger made her feel.

Monrose crossed back into Arnos Vale. He moved among his people, speaking softly, encouraging them. When he reached Sinclair he crouched beside him, their heads together.

Vic was thinking about that, about the bond they shared. He envied that closeness. They were comrades, loyal and close in a way he doubted he'd ever experienced. Instead, Vic thought about Michelle and Stan. About what his duty to them was, when a scream, huge and piercing, tore across the air.

Vic swayed where he stood, sick to his stomach.

A very human scream, rich with pain and nearby—beyond the walls of the graveyard but not far.

Monrose stepped over. "Steady now," Monrose said. "It'll be soon."

"Sergeant," Sinclair said, "Time you were on your way."

Monrose nodded. He grasped each bottle of Jim Beam by the neck and faded away into the shadow of the obelisks. Not fleeing, Vic knew, but *hunting*.

Petra had smelt the stench of death many times. It filled her senses, bloody and metallic.

Beauty seemed to glow with an impossible light, even in the shroud of darkfall. He glowed with power. The owner had whipped himself into a frenzy with Anna's death. Spilled blood always made them stronger.

The mounted strigoi rode forward, their chargehands pushing the workers before them. They came to the gates of the cemetery. The black wrought-iron stood like lines of spears between two large concrete gatehouses. At the Ogre's command, strigoi and workers alike swarmed over the iron fences either side of the gates. They either struggled or sprang over the six-foot barrier, the crowd growing on either side.

Faced with the gates, the strigoi's mounts closed slowly. Like elephants they lumbered, lurching and swaying until their pawlike forearms and heads pressed against the iron. Tongues lolling from their idiot faces, they leaned harder. Iron protested, the pressure building and still the beasts bent forward. Their breath rumbled in their deep chests with effort and finally the links of the chain shrieked and snapped apart.

Surging forward, the mounts scattered before them a loose barricade of wardrobes, planks and benches. All of them, strigoi, hands and workers flooded into Arnos Vale.

Beauty led them, alongside the other mounted strigoi. When the owners moved off the path, even slightly, they hissed at one another, disturbed by the ground in some way. But there was a route they could follow. The owners moved instinctively, leading their army deeper into the graveyard.

Beauty called out to a chargehand, his voice chittering and sibilant.

In turn, the chargehand said, "I speak for the owners," calling out ahead.

Petra couldn't see who the hand called to, but she guessed that people hid here from the strigoi. She imagined slipping away and finding them. She wondered about that even as one of the owner's mounts turned and clicked its teeth at her. Then it nudged her, sending her sprawling. And that made Petra think again.

From the shadows of Arnos Vale, a man shouted back. "Who are you?"

The chargehand said, "Surrender. All of you, immediately. You cannot escape the owners. You cannot escape the darkfall."

Beauty hissed with delight.

* * *

Vic's anger seared him at talking to a human traitor.

"The owners want the one called Sinclair," the traitor said. "They will sacrifice him. The rest of you may be permitted to live. As slaves. This is the best you can hope for. The future belongs to their kind now."

Vic glanced at Sinclair. Sinclair nodded to Vic to continue. The strigoi passed between the piled furniture of either side of the path. They stayed off the consecrated ground of the gardens of rest and turned their slave army to face them, forming a crescent. There were so many of them.

"My friend has something to say about that," Vic said. As he said it, he realised that Sinclair would have never been his friend in any world but this one.

The army appeared to be led by two strigoi on horseback. This was the first time Vic had seen the strigoi. One had hair as white as Sinclair's, but he looked far more ancient.

Vic stared with horror at the monsters the strigoi rode. The riders surveyed the graveyard, looking satisfied. They ignored the piles of furniture and scavenged wood that stood behind them.

The white haired strigoi said, "You built a city that now stands abandoned. Your people flee us. You live in a slaughterhouse, waiting for your owners to claim you." His voice was leathery and old. He smiled wetly at Sinclair, his eyes shining as he singled him out.

Sinclair raised his Smith & Wesson, sighting steadily, and his right arm slightly bent.

He shot at the old strigoi.

In response, the strigoi hissed with amusement at his

feeble threat.

Sinclair said to Vic. "Mr Edmond. You better shout—so that Monrose definitely knows I've signalled him."

Automatically, Vic obeyed. He shouted at the strigoi: "Come get us, you *bastards*!"

If Monrose threw the first Molotov, Vic didn't see it. But a sheet of fire exploded behind the strigoi in the darkness. The stacked wood took light, licking and flickering with red tongues of flame.

Vic heard Monrose. "Welcome to our world, *owner*." He shouted across the graveyard as the flames raced from behind the strigoi and into them. The strigoi were caught in a channel between the fire and the consecrated ground.

Monrose threw the second bottle, shattering it and scattering another burst of fire across the next bank of gathered wood.

The pale faces ringing the strigoi, captives and allies, snapped round, looking each way at once. The humans moved, coming forward onto the consecrated ground and away from the dense cloud of smoke and the licking, crackling flames as the wood caught. They could step into the gardens of rest, tripping over the tombstones but otherwise unaffected. The strigoi could not.

Monrose's people ran forward, tipping plastic petrol cans into the strigoi's ranks. Faster now, and much hotter, the fire raced upwards, spreading through the prisoners and strigoi both. There was so much light and heat that Vic ducked back from the roar and speed of it. The smoke off the fire eddied and stank.

* * *

The air blazed bright yellow before Petra.

Screaming, the workers surged away. Bodies tumbled past her. Workers, chargehands, and strigoi, all boxed between the consecrated ground and the bonfires that seemed to explode all around them. Smoke, rich and dark as unmilked chocolate swirled out of the fire, thicker than the mist and the stench of burning.

Petra had heard screams before, heard begging for mercy, but nothing like this. Workers spun around her, their shifts alight, their arms wind-milling through the flames. The smell changed, like frying steaks on a hob. That was human flesh, cracking and splitting. Choking on the stench, Petra was shoved aside as people fled past her.

The strigoi screamed with rage and fear. The proud voices of attackers, of winners, turned high and frightened.

"No, no," the Ogre shouted. Petra was surprised at his anguish. He had learned that much from his slaves.

The Ogre tried to push Beauty's mount, turning its head from the fire. Terrified, the deformed creature swung away. Then it swung back and its huge hand slapped the Ogre. The hand landed with such force that it snapped the Ogre's head right round. He sprawled, face stove in like a squashed fruit. Then his red robes danced with flames as the fire engulfed his body.

The fire spread everywhere, jumping like a snarling dog. The strigoi and their chargehands rolled and screamed, their flesh aflame. The smell deepened, flooding her nose, as the dead writhed and split, cooking in their juices.

Strigoi fled in all directions. Beauty, caught in the surge of bodies, whipped his mount and began trampling his way free.

Petra ran. Ran as the other workers were running, but *into* the fire, not away. She lunged through a golden river of light to Beauty and his mewling beast.

Flames licked at her feet but their bright touch energised her. She vaulted off the burning ground. Almost to her surprise, she found the sharpened pipe in her fist, its point ready for Beauty. When she met the ancient owner's stare, his eyes were patient and alien as an arctic bird's. With a fighter's poise, he turned his mount, side-stepping Petra as her pipe came down in an arc. The gaping face of the mount turned, the creature bucking from the flames as Petra tumbled into them.

Petra fell through heat and noise and the stink of burning. She twisted and kept with Beauty as he danced away. She slammed her sharpened pipe into his skinny thigh. His eyes widened—with surprise rather than pain, as if he had forgotten what feeling was like. He jeered at her, his mouth a red kiss.

Petra, tangled in the leather of the mount's stirrups, gripped the saddle. Beauty raked her with his long fingers. Sharp as diamonds, they sliced through her arms, her ear and face. The pain was exquisite and needle-fine.

From the ground, fire raced up Petra's back, too hot to bear, but she clung on, dragging the saddle down into the sea of fire beneath them. And with it, Beauty himself. The red kiss of Beauty's mouth widened and his voice rose into its violin wail. But now it was a scream of pain.

The fire on Petra's back, flew over her shift, then spat as it ate her flesh. She screamed too. She screamed Anna's name and pulled Beauty's hard body tight to her. She screamed in defiance at the strigoi and their world of darkfall.

The flames took her, took Beauty and his beast as well and all around Petra the strigoi writhed and screamed, their flesh running red and black in the river of gold.

She fell into the inferno, her hair on fire. Her flesh shrivelled away, but in her left fist she clung to Beauty's emaciated arm. She pulled him to her, touching an owner for the only time, as the fire ate them both.

Vic watched the blaze. Its heat beat back at him as the strigoi rolled and died, bathed in red flames. Vic forgot to hold his breath. Forgot until the stench of burning filled his face and his stomach roiled.

The strigoi's squealing pierced the air, even over the crackle and splutter of the fire. And counterpoint to it came the cries of men and women caught with them.

War, Vic saw. War made few distinctions.

He glanced over at Monrose. The American had crossed back to them and stood by Sinclair. They watched what they'd done.

"Victory," Monrose said.

Seeing Vic's face, Sinclair said, "It's the cost of winning."

Vic stared, his horror mingled with relief. The strigoi and their slaves twisted and burned together.

The cost of winning, Vic thought. Then, *Michelle. Stan.*

He might find them now. Might spend a lifetime with them.

Something struck Vic's neck. He flinched before it hit again and he realised it was rain. A black rain, falling gently. He stared into the sky, blinking. Was the darkfall weaker, less boundless? But it still hung over them, oppressive and pestilential.

"You killed the strigoi," Vic said to Monrose.

"That we did. Some of 'em, anyway."

"They're not human," Sinclair said. "They are stronger and longer lived, but that doesn't make them smarter than us. They're animals." He gave Vic a look. "Remember that."

"Is it over?"

Sinclair shook his head. "There's always more. But we fought back. And we go on fighting back."

Not over, yet this fight had cost so much. Vic hoped that the ghosts of the strigoi's victims would forgive him for paying this price.

Sinclair slid his pistol out from his jacket and slapped it into Monrose's palm. "Sergeant, surviving traitors, if you please?"

Monrose nodded. "You'll be all right here? On your own?"

Sinclair smiled and turned to Vic. "I believe Mr Edmond is with us now. Is that right, Vic?"

Monrose watched him calmly. "Fighters," was all he said.

Vic thought of Stan and Michelle. He wanted nothing more than to return to them. But he also knew about the strigoi, and he knew how to kill them.

He gathered himself, inhaling deeply of the foul air. He nodded to Monrose and stepped over to stand at Sinclair's side. With them. A comrade and a fighter now.

Dev Agarwal

Dev Agarwal writes dark fantasy, near future science fiction and horror. He has published fiction in *Albedo One, Aeon*, the British Fantasy Society's *Horizons, Hungur, Aoife's Kiss*, and forthcoming in *Mithila Review* in India.

Dev is an associate editor for the science fiction magazine *Albedo One.* He also writes non fiction for a variety of websites and for the British Science Fiction Association's *Focus* and *Vector* magazines.

Dev has worked in a variety of jobs, including in a dysfunctional department of the British government, fitness instructor and complaints investigator.

Dev's fantasy and horror writing draws on history, often the ancient world. *Darkfall* is part of a linked series of stories about vampires that span different historical epochs, including the stories *Ghosts*, set during World War One, and *Domina*, in Ancient Rome.

Unwelcome

AMANDA STAPLES

Standing in my favourite part of the house, I am looking out of a trefoil squint window. The old chapel is out of my eyeline but I can see the edges of fir trees that form the boundary, across my garden and out over fields. When I stand here I can breathe again. I feel safe.

I moved to Milford to start over. It's a chocolate-box English village in the Cotswolds. Everything Brighton isn't. And that's what makes it perfect for a fresh start. As far as prejudice of the local's goes, well, much as it's irritating, I'm almost grateful for the lack of interest and intrusion. I don't want people knowing my business. I don't want questions asked. The whole point of coming here is to get a clean slate. I don't want to rake up the past. I refuse to let the villagers' attitude affect me. It's because I'm an interloper; a townie. That's all it is. Well, I'm stubborn and I'm here to stay. But I will admit to feeling a bit lonely some nights.

People at least acknowledge me now when I walk into the pub. A nod. A grunt if they are feeling especially sociable. The first time I set foot in the Crown and Cushion it was like one of those Westerns where the doors swing shut and there's silence and tumbleweed. All that was missing was someone chewing tobacco and spitting on the floor.

"You're still here then," Mick says, pushing my gin and tonic across the bar. I wonder if drinking 'a townie drink' doesn't help, but I cannot abide ale.

"Apparently so," I reply, with a wry smile as I sip my drink.

I've been in the house three weeks now and he's the second person to talk to me, as opposed to grunt. I half expected them to form a posse and chase me out of the village with pitchforks. They managed to see off the person who was trying to buy the old chapel next door to me. I considered buying the chapel with its gothic windows and ornately carved wooden door but it's so densely surrounded by trees it feels claustrophobic, and then there's the gravestones. Not that there's much of anyone left—a few rat droppings, bones and rotted coffin parts per grave—but I don't want a graveyard as a garden. You can't exactly sunbathe on a tombstone, can you? Well, I wouldn't. So, I bought the old parsonage instead, which is light and airy with breathtaking views and no graveyard. Apart from the pet cemetery, which exists in the plans but I have yet to discover amongst the overgrown brambles.

This is my third scintillating conversation with Mick. The first time he spoke to me other than serving me at the bar he said, "They'll not like you living there." This was the day my offer had been accepted on the property, and I'd popped into the friendly-looking local for a celebratory drink. Well, so much for that. But their pigheadedness was not about to dissuade me from buying my dream house.

Even the estate agent tried to put me off. The place had been on his books for over two years, you'd think he'd be glad to get shot of it.

Such an absolute steal; tens of thousands knocked off the asking price. I cheekily offered low and am beyond thrilled at it being accepted, albeit it's a doer-upper, to say the least. But I like a challenge. Four bedrooms, drawing room, sitting room, sun room, flagstone floors, Aga. Funny how the clergy had the best houses back in the day. It's like something out of a classic novel, but not quite a Poldark or Downton Abbey 'Lord of the Manor'. It lacks climbing roses around the door. Which reminds me, I must do something about that ivy.

Dilapidated though it is, I am confident that with the right help, I can restore it to its former glory. Down-at-heel the estate agent called it. Rotten wooden window frames, panes smashed from local kids throwing stones, grime and dust.

Why do people always say abandoned houses are spooky or haunted? Ridiculous. The estate agent asked me if I was bothered by my neighbours. He whispered the word and nodded at the chapel. I rolled my eyes and asked how could I be when they were dead and that at least I could make all the noise I liked. He said something about being careful not to make enough noise to wake the dead which I think was supposed to be a joke, but he was so jittery it was hard to tell. He wouldn't even come in, just gave me the keys and told me to knock myself out. I nearly did when a chandelier came crashing down in the sitting room inches away from me. I'm sure in its full working glory it had been spectacular with all those glittering crystal drops. Awful shame, it's quite beyond repair. But doubtless the bolt was rusty and the movement of me walking about above it probably loosened it.

Unlike that pathetic estate agent, I refuse to be swayed by this ludicrous local legend. Scaremongering, that's all it is. I'm sure they've put off countless buyers before me. It's all bollocks. Do you know how I know? Because there are no two versions of events that are the same. The estate agent, Mick in the pub, and the woman in the local shop all have differing stories and are vague. Poppycock as my dear old Pa would say. It's jealousy. They are envious that I can afford to buy the place. Even at its knockdown price, I doubt any of them would have the finances. Well tough. I'm not going to apologise for the fact that I can afford it. I worked hard for my money and I fought hard in my divorce. I've earned this house and I'm going to bloody well live in it.

Getting it fixed up is laborious. I wanted to be in within weeks, but it's been months. Nobody local will set foot in the place. It's preposterous. I mean, honestly, we are talking about grown men.

Work is sporadic and shoddy. The sash windows are supposed to have been renewed but one near decapitated me when it freed itself as I leaned out to paint the windowsill.

The chimneys were supposed to be swept but when I nodded off one night in the sitting room, reading, I woke gasping. Smoke pouring from the fireplace, the room engulfed in what tasted like smog.

This is what happens when you are a woman alone. People take advantage of you. And it's not like I can be here all the time to supervise the workers.

They all claim they've carried out the work properly, of course. Like the plumber, who swore blind he'd fitted that shower perfectly after I'd complained it had scolded me—I mean literally burned me. One minute it's fine, the next, I am dowsed in searing hot water. My scalp is still tender. And my buttocks. Thank goodness I was facing away from the showerhead.

Six months on, the villagers have stopped saying I should leave. They nod and grunt at me still, and smile sometimes, but now they have taken to looking at me in a peculiar way. If I didn't know better I'd say it looks like pity, but it can't be. I ignore it. They look at me the way people do when you've been bereaved and they don't know what to say. Odd. Anyway, what do I care? I stay in my lovely house and cook and paint and read, and I'm happy. Though I do need to tackle the garden. I've been putting that off for far too long. I'm sure there are some real delights under the brambles, bindweed and nettles that I can free up. And I want to find that pet cemetery. Apparently, the parson set aside a piece of ground for all the village children to bury their dead pets. I think that's a lovely idea. I remember seeing one at a National Trust house years ago with little wooden crosses for the household dogs in days gone by. I wonder what names I shall find, if the grave-markers have survived, that is.

* * *

It's the night after the dream when they come. I've finally made a friend—Sarah at the tea rooms. I'm starting to feel like I am, well, not fitting in as such, but perhaps being accepted more. I sit drinking tea while she potters, we are on our own. It's that quiet late afternoon period just before closing. Sarah is also an ex-townie so we bond over our 'lack of being a local'.

"But someone in the village must own a lurcher," I say. "I saw it run across the lawn when I was I was looking out of the squint window."

"Perhaps it was a shadow or a trick of the light through the branches of the trees?"

I give her a withering look. "And that tabby cat was back again last night. I don't know how it's getting in. It must sneak in when I open the door and lie low. I swear I can hear it scratching at the back door, but when I go to shoo it away it's already in the kitchen by the Aga. Perhaps it's feral. It never lets me touch it."

"Perhaps it's shy or was abused, give it time," Sarah says.

"It's not shy. It stalks about like it owns the place and hisses at me when I go near it. I don't want to give it time. I don't want it in the house."

"Well, Mabel in the shop would know about strays," Sarah suggests.

"I've asked her. She says no-ones missing a cat. Sometimes it sits on that crumbled wall on the boundary between the fir trees and just stares at me. I can see it from the kitchen window."

Sarah puts a plate in front of me then turns the door

sign to *Closed*.

"Oh, my favourite, you spoil me with your leftovers."

"Has anything else peculiar happened?" she asks as she busies herself tidying chairs.

"A stray cat and a lost lurcher are not peculiar. I've been having odd dreams though. The last one was bizarre," I say, chewing on a fruit flapjack. "You know when a dream is so vivid it feels real—you wake up believing it's happened?"

"I suppose, yeah." Sarah shrugs as she slices up banana bread and wraps it in foil. She will take this to the old manor house that had been turned into a nursing home. No-one ever goes on about that being haunted; perhaps because it's full of the living dead.

I continue, "I dreamed my bedroom was frozen. In the middle of summer! I woke shivering and put my foot out of the bed and the floor was a sheet of ice, so cold it burned my bare skin. Icicles hung from a four-poster bed. When I properly awoke, my teeth were chattering. How weird is that?"

Sarah stops slicing the cake. "You don't have a four-poster bed, do you?"

"No. Like I said, it was a dream."

"Are you in the master bedroom overlooking the old pond?"

"Yes, of course. Biggest room, best view."

Sarah hesitates then places the knife down and leans on the counter. "Look, Faye. I know you don't want to hear this but—"

"Oh Sarah, not you too. Please don't start spouting all this local legend rubbish. I thought you were better than that," I snap, furious with her.

"You need to leave," Sarah says.

"Look, I'm sorry I bit at you. I'm just tired and fed up with—"

"Not my shop, Faye. The house."

I sigh, roll my eyes and shake my head, disappointed with her. "Please don't start spouting all that blasted local legend crap. I don't know why everyone is so keen to perpetuate this myth."

"Because it's legend for a reason. It's not myth. I'll prove it to you." Sarah comes out from behind the counter. "Show me your feet."

"No! Don't be ridiculous."

But Sarah is already bending down. "I'm serious."

"Oh, for pity's sake," I mutter toeing off my sandals, just to prove her wrong and not wanting to fight with one of few friendly faces in the village. I hope my feet smell. That'll serve her right.

Sarah examines the soles of my feet then gasps. She stands up so quickly her hip catches an adjacent table sending soiled crockery crashing to the floor.

I frown at her and turn my foot. A red mark runs along the left one. I had noticed my foot had felt sore earlier but put it down to the nettles.

"I was gardening yesterday, stupidly in sandals. I hadn't meant to do much then I started uncovering that dear little pet cemetery and I ended up wading in to all sorts. It's just an irritation from pollen or sting from nettles, that's all," I say, replacing my shoes.

Sarah doesn't say anything and now she is looking at me in the way that all the other villagers do.

Livid, I scrape my chair back and stand up. "You're the only sane one in the village. Get a bloody grip will you?" I say as I flounce out. I'm so cross with her I forget to pay but when I go back the following morning she's closed. Milford is one of those dying-breed villages that closes in its entirety on a Wednesday. Even the pub.

The damned electrics have gone on the blink again. The electrician said it was an untraceable fault. What on earth is that supposed to mean? Luckily, it's light enough and warm enough to sit and read in the garden, the bit I'd tidied anyway; a section of lawn between the old pond and the pet cemetery. I'd unearthed some of the pet cemetery and stood the little wooden crosses back up. A lot of the names were faded. Scrag, was the only one that had survived. I can just imagine what that animal had looked like. No sign of the cat tonight.

Around nine o'clock I go inside. I decide to sit in the window seat, listen to Bach and enjoy a glass of wine. That's when I see them.

The villagers advance on me mob-handed. Carrying torches, guns, scythes and other weapons. Flailing their arms. Shouting. I can't make out the words at first, I am too shocked.

"Leave!"

"Get out!"

I cannot believe my eyes and stare dumbfounded for a moment as they near.

"Get out! Get out!"

Coming to my senses, I leap from the seat to fetch my

phone and call the police. My bag is in the kitchen. I try to recall if I'd locked the front and back doors. What if they force their way in before help arrives? What if the local police are in cahoots with them?

I turn the door knob and yank. I don't remember shutting the sitting room door, but I must have. It doesn't budge. I try again, swearing, sweating. Clammy palms sliding on the shiny brass knob. The glow of the torches brighter, the shouting louder.

"Get out! Get out!"

Bile rises and I begin hyperventilating. I have to get out. I have to.

The room is plunged into darkness. Like someone has turned the lamps off. But they hadn't been on. As I tug frantically at the door, from the corner of my eye, I realise I can no longer see the torches. I let go of the door knob and turn. The window is completely covered in ivy.

I am having trouble breathing—panic. Also, because the room is filling with smoke billowing from the fireplace. Grey, gritty, sooty smoke chokes me, making my eyes stream.

Something tickles my bare feet and I scream. I look down, squinting through tears to see a tabby tail winding around my calves. The cat trips me as I stumble in a vain attempt to escape. He hisses as I tumble, then disappears into the smoke. I feel a constriction around my thighs, then my waist. I look down to see ivy snaking up my body.

I lay crying and coughing until the breath is squeezed from my lungs by the climbing ivy. I can hear men hammering on the front door, glass breaking, more shouts. I realise they won't get to me in time.

The last thing I hear as the ivy curls around my ears, up my nostrils, across my eyes, a whisper, "You're not welcome."

AMANDA STAPLES

Amanda Staples is fascinated by the workings of the mind and has a minor obsession with death. This led her to become a hypnotherapist in lieu of an undertaker.

Her writing is fuelled by pots of tea and drams of whisky. Her work has featured in anthologies and various literary magazines and has been recorded for podcasts and youtube. She self-published a recipe book and is currently indulging her novel writing ambition. Her play *Weston on a Sunday* has been staged in Croydon and Bristol. She has read at Bath Lit Fringe Fest, Bristol Lit Fest, Talking Tales and Writers Unchained events in Bristol, and Stroud Short Stories.

When not writing, she is felting, pom-pomming, reading, or chatting to her anthropomorphised dogs. You can follow her on Facebook @scribestaples and Twitter @scribestaples1

Unforgotten

KEN SHINN

"**P**atience," Ben Reiterman would often explain to his house guests after a good evening's drinking, "is an undeniable virtue in hunting. Consider the cat outside the mouse hole. But ultimately, the greatest virtue in hunting is strength. Consider the great white shark against the tunny fish."

If the brandy had flowed freely enough and the guest was honoured enough, then Reiterman would invite him into his study, and show him the ranks of handsomely-mounted heads: lion, tiger, zebra, grizzly, bison, on and on in a showcase of dead pelts, glass eyes and sawdust.

Often, his guests would enquire as to whether the use of high-powered rifles meant that the hunt was never exactly fair. Reiterman would usually respond by challenging them to a hand-to-hand knife fight. Only two had ever taken him up on it. The first had lost his nerve at the last moment and ran out of the door with Reiterman's cheery call of, "Fucking queer!" ringing in his ears. The second had bloodied him several times before the wounds that he inflicted on her had taken their toll, and she'd conceded. What a woman. They'd enjoyed a passionate if brief relationship before she ran out on him. No real stomach for the hunt.

His life was generally good: independently wealthy, a gym-toned and hardened body, several Hemingway first editions on his shelves, one of them even signed. Not to mention an armoury that Rambo would envy. He lived for the adrenaline rush and the sudden death, and he revelled in every moment of it.

There was only one thing missing. A bull elephant head for his collection. The largest, strongest land animal of them all, and one which would make for a damned impressive trophy. After researching his options, he decided on two things. Firstly, he needed to head to the Congo Basin, and hunt an African forest elephant— something about the primal vitality of a jungle hunt appealed to him. Secondly, he was going to hunt it alone. The battle needed to be fought one-on-one, and with no potential bleeding-heart witnesses. He knew people who could get him there and back for the right price, and no awkward questions asked—a blessing in such damnably politically-correct times as these. Papa Hemingway would have approved, he was sure.

He braced himself against the hard African soil, hidden from the scorching sun by the cool shade of the massive trees, focusing on the huge grey beast several hundred yards away. The bull had ambled away from the herd for whatever pointless needs elephants did, in a downright provincial manner. The animal would be on its own: a clear target, and easy to track if anything did go awry. A clean kill would be preferable, but all he had to do was wound it to ensure a trail could be followed.

He unscrewed his canteen, took a long swallow of already warm water. Brandy would have tasted better, but he'd save that until he'd triumphed. Socketing the .577 T-Rex firmly into his shoulder, he pushed the brim of his hat slightly higher, and lingeringly lined up his sights square in the middle of that broad expanse of deeply-wrinkled forehead.

A shaved second before he squeezed the trigger, a sharp pain yelled out in his left calf. He jolted involuntarily as he fired, and the .577 Tyrannosaur bullet's path shifted accordingly. It finally buried itself in the side of the bull's chest. The beast trumpeted in agony, and charged blunderingly into the nearest stand of trees, snapping off branches and stomping wet ground as it disappeared. Reiterman smashed the bottle-green horsefly on his leg. Wiping the smeared remains away, he sprang to his feet in pursuit. Clear splashes of blood showed bright red among the green. The familiar and ever-welcome rush hit him as he levelled his weapon and pursued his quarry, deeper into the forest.

Ahead he heard the crashes and trumpets of pain as his quarry blundered onward into the undergrowth. The spoor was almost unnecessary, so he lingered for a pleasing moment to properly reload his rifle and check the edge of the machete at his hip one more time. Since the kill was now all but certain, he allowed himself a healthy swig of cognac. There'd be more soon, after all. Fully prepared, he charged with growing joy, relishing the way his strong body effortlessly whipped through low branches that lashed, then yielded to his passage. As he often did, he felt a gleeful link with the prehistoric hunters of days long past, and welcomed the swift descent of the red mist before his eyes.

So swept up in the moment, he failed to notice the sudden drop ahead of him. He charged into suddenly empty air and thumped heavily to the rockier ground below. The fall wasn't more than three or four feet at most, but he landed badly. A spear of pain stabbed into his right leg, and he stifled his involuntary roar of agony.

Cursing, he shifted carefully to a sitting position, and probed his ankle. The responding angry throb told an unwelcome story. No bones appeared to be broken. He probably had a bad sprain – but that was nothing. Ernest would have sneered at such a minor setback. After reaching into an equipment pouch, he removed and swallowed several painkillers, chasing them down with more warm water. Those, and adrenaline, should be more than enough to allow the chase to continue. Bracing himself on his rifle butt, he rose and slowly took a few experimental steps. Each one brought a fresh shard of pain, but it was nothing that he couldn't handle, and the foot held. So, a hobbling pursuit. Not the most elegant, but it would still get the job done. A grim smile crossed his face as he resumed tracking the blood.

The agony in his right foot dulled steadily during the hours that followed, as he limped steadily onward. The bull, wounded as it was, still doubtless had a good lead on him. The trail of blood grew ever more difficult to follow, but the beast's blundering flight had left plenty more evidence in broken branches, smashed patches of grass, and clear footprints in occasional muddy patches of the ground, which had become steadily drier and rockier as Reiterman pursued. The trees were gradually thinning out around him, and he marked how the terrain ahead was beginning a long but gentle incline, leading down between great cliffs on either side. The pass through them was clearly still wide enough for an elephant to pass, though—and sure enough, the sandy soil had been recently disturbed, and here and there bright spots of drying blood still showed. Reiterman paused, stooped, touched a spot, and wiped it slowly onto his tongue, relishing the salty, animal taste of the life that was soon to be taken. He stood upright and tested his ankle once more. He'd need both hands free for the gun, when the time came.

Good. He could only move at a slow hobble without the impromptu crutch, but that was enough. He'd keep using the rifle to get down this slope. It had to give way to flat ground eventually, and from what he could discern the cliffs were not just on either side of him, but straight ahead at the end of his trail. The injured bull had made a mistake, and was doubtless suffering from its wound, confused and probably frozen with fear and pain—and it now had no way back out. His trophy was all but assured.

The journey down the defile took longer than he'd hoped. Not only did his complaining ankle continue to ache, to the point where he paused on occasion and carelessly swallowed more brandy to lessen its significance, but the trail just didn't bloody end. It twisted and turned, presumably following the path of some long-gone river, leading steadily downward. The shade of the cliffs provided some respite, but the early afternoon sun was high and merciless. Reiterman removed his bush hat momentarily to swipe sticky sweat from his forehead. He found himself wondering idly if he was hallucinating mildly—a combination of alcohol, painkillers and the sheer heat could be doing that, he mused, and the descent seemed endless. He debated resting briefly, then shook the notion away. That would be weakness, and he was not weak. His own strength, willpower and bloodlust would be more than enough to overcome such trifles.

At last, his journey came to an end. The path opened out onto a flat, hard-packed plain, scattered with great boulders and patches of sun-bleached stones. The great cliffs, split with enormous crevasses, surrounded it—as he'd known there were no other ways out. Raising the rifle to his shoulder once more, he scanned the killing-ground. And sure enough, there was the bull. It stood by one of the largest rocks, its leathery flank stained with drying blood. He listened in satisfaction as it sputtered and snorted. The elephant hadn't been wounded mortally, or maybe even seriously—but it had been damaged enough to cause a degree of blood loss and shortness of breath. It became weaker: he became stronger. Its eyes were fixed on him, but it made no attempt to charge him, or to attempt some idiotic escape. Well, Reiterman thought wryly, they are supposed to be wise... Slowly, deliberately, he paced forward, T-Rex loaded and ready.

His dry mouth started to water in anticipation, and his swollen, tortured ankle ceased to matter.

Something was... not wrong, but somehow off. It took him several more seconds before he realised. The plain was silent. No birdsong, no rush of wind, no chatter of monkeys or chitter of crickets. Apart from the laboured pants of breath from both man and beast, no sound could be heard. A momentary uncertainty nagged at the back of his mind, and he smashed it casually. This was the time. Never letting his gaze waver, he raised the gun decisively and took his aim, squarely between the bull's eyes. It had arrived, that perfect moment. The victor and the vanquished. The hunter and the prey. The quick and the dead.

There was an odd look in the animal's eyes. Reiterman had expected pain and fear, but none of that showed in its expression. It looked contemplative, cold. Like a scientist studying a specimen. Despite himself, the hunter shifted backwards a step, and his foot came down on one of those whitened stones.

It was when the stone crunched under his boot that he realised that something was very wrong. He looked closer. The thing had been hollow, and his foot had smashed it partially open. A sudden suspicion made his blood freeze. He turned the stone over carefully with his toe, and found himself gazing at grinning teeth and empty eye sockets. Human eye sockets.

Awareness caused him to look more closely at the scattered patches of white stones. Now, he saw the torn remnants of clothing and kit. The smashed, useless rifles. The silent legacy of skulls, ribs, femurs, ulnas, intact and shattered. Forebears. Dozens of them. Their mortal remains apparently gathered like so many trophies. His mind reeled and his vision hazed. With a quick, desperate shake of his head, he attempted to throw off the shock, and hefted his rifle in suddenly palsied fingers, raising his gaze once more.

The bull was no longer alone. Enough elephants to call a proper herd had appeared from the various crevasses in the cliffs, silently as ghosts. Reiterman recalled the amazing quietness with which such huge creatures could move on occasion. There was still nothing impossible about what had happened. In a few more moments, normality would return.

The animals gathered together to form a silent line of towering menace. His quick estimate told him that there had to be at least thirty. He'd seen larger herds, but never a number like this moving with apparent common purpose. He met their collective gaze, and now he saw not only that same calm scrutiny that the bull had given him, but what could only be the intensity of steadily-rising, massed fury. That couldn't be. These were dumb animals. More intelligent than most, but surely not comparable to a man in either brainpower or emotions. That wasn't natural!

His rifle was his staff and comfort. Bracing himself once more, he attempted to take proper aim at his bull again. If he killed just one, then that would hopefully frighten the rest enough to scare them off. It was unfortunate, then, that several of the elephants chose that moment to charge at him en masse. Sudden furious trumpeting split the still, stiflingly hot air, and Reiterman threw himself aside with a startled yell, desperate to evade the sudden stampede. As he landed heavily, his T-Rex was knocked from his grip, flying to land well beyond his reach. Instinctively, he bellied towards it in dawning terror.

He was within three feet of it when an enormous flat foot stamped down, smashing and splintering thousands of dollars' worth of high-range ordnance with a single dismissive blow. The elephant, slightly ahead of its fellows, stared down at him with bloody murder in its eyes. With a sudden burst of frantic energy, Reiterman managed to scramble to his feet and out of the elephant's direct path. His hand fumbled at his belt for the great machete that hung there, seeking defence, any defence. As his fingers brushed the hilt, a trunk lashed out from behind him with alarming accuracy, slapping his arm away, jarring his shoulder with fresh pain. Another trunk curled round his waist with surprising speed, and he gazed helplessly as that prehensile appendage precisely snatched at his belt and tore the knife away, flinging it dismissively far off and away. Fear roared up in him like brushfire. He began a stumbling retrograde, facing the beasts in front of him as much as he could. If he could only reach the slope, he might be able to beat a successful retreat. Hide. Reconsider. Retaliate.

His back hit something solid, massive. Alive. An elephant had circled off from the group to cut off his escape. He whirled to face it, and saw not one but three of the creatures blocking him. Turning in a bewildered three-sixty, he realised that they'd trapped him at the centre of a large, organised ring. They were working together. His sanity almost collapsed under the terror of that realisation. And around him... how many skeletons? How many lives taken? How many other hunters had preceded him in all-too-ignorant confidence down onto this killing floor?

How many more would follow?

Several of the herd broke off from the ring to charge him from all sides. There was no way that he could hope to avoid them all. He threw himself aside once more, hoping to find a clear way, but only succeeded in smashing more breath out of himself as he hit the earth. The stamping beasts lowered their heads as they ran, the great tusks opening savage, bleeding gashes in his arms, legs, even his face. Half-blind, he groped to his feet once more. He saw a gap, a small but definite gap, in the ranks, and survival instinct kicked in as he saw the crevasse. Maybe they wouldn't, hopefully couldn't, follow him back there if it twisted and narrowed enough. The roar of adrenalised blood in his ears drowned out the continued trumpeting. None of the other pain—his gashes, the bruised shoulder, even that bloody ankle— mattered any more. All that mattered was the sudden, wild hope that had risen in his heart. The speed of his shambling run was impressive. Inside the next twenty seconds, he'd charged head down through that narrow window of opportunity, his eyes fixed steadily onward and upward at his goal, his legs pumping powerfully as he gained the shelter. Now, at last, he had a chance.

Hope died there. The wide walls were closing in swiftly. Too swiftly. The passage was too narrow for him to head in more than a dozen feet at most and, as he turned, he realised that the space behind him was still more than wide enough for a single elephant to follow him in. He was going to die here. Barely aware of the piss suddenly rilling down his legs, he tried to grab back the last shreds of his courage, his strength. If he was going to die, then he'd look Death straight in the eye, and laugh...

The cordon of elephants approached quietly. As they reached the way to Reiterman, they paused. Their great heads swayed slowly back and forth, as if talking among themselves. Then, they nodded in unison. Moving almost reverently off to each side, they let one of their number through.

The drying blood on the flank told Reiterman all that he needed to know. The bull that he'd injured had been chosen as his executioner. The beast moved steadily forward, its bulk blotting out the sunlight ahead, its steady snorts echoing from the sides of the trap. Reiterman kept his gaze locked on it, knowing that the fury, the hatred in the animal's own was all too real. All too knowing. The great head loomed nearer, its sharp tusks catching the dim light.

Reiterman opened his mouth to roar out that last, defiant laugh at the exact moment that the bull's head lunged forward, and the great spears of ivory punched through his rib cage and deep into his chest, smashing bones, pulping organs, spilling blood, and all that emerged from his mouth was a gush of mortal scarlet. His death was not instantaneous. He had time to feel the crushing agony of his many wounds for a long minute as his reluctant soul refused to escape its host. And time to feel, even more severely, that greater pain of his own failure.

Finally, the bull drew back, his trunk dragging the smashed corpse carefully after him. He pulled it with slow, careful patience over to a clear patch of dusty soil, where he dropped it and, turning, unceremoniously defecated over it.

Turning to his fellows, he met their eyes in turn, sensing their approval and their satisfaction. He was injured, but he would heal: and, with the help of his friends, he had dealt out the appropriate sentence to the slayer. With a quiet feeling of contentment in his heart, he led his fellows off to disappear once more into the comfort of the wilderness, leaving the shattered and befouled shell of the killer under the vault of the blue heavens to await the predations of beast and element.

The Elephants' Graveyard had a fresh memorial.

KEN SHINN

Ken Shinn is now 54 years old, and still lives in Bristol with his two marvellous cats, Smeagol and Helium. He is finally, after many pledges, on the verge of completing his first novel, an expansion of his first published short story, *Case Of The Vapours*.

He remains primarily interested in horror and supernatural fiction, with recent short stories appearing in the collections *Mummy Knows Best* and *The Hotwells Horror and Other Stories*. While planning more of those, he is also due to have work published soon in *The UNIT Fannual, 1974* and the upcoming celebrations of David Bowie and Target's Doctor Who novelisations, *Me And The Starman* and *You On Target*.

And he's also very fond of elephants.

Graveyard Shift

JAY MILLINGTON

Intense white light blinds me, but I'm unable to close my eyes.

"This one's functioning," says an educated male voice in an even tone.

"Stick him in the store," says another.

I wake, standing, with a cover over my bowed head. I am incapable of movement, not even a blink. Someone behind walks away. On the lower periphery of my fixed vision, I make out my clothes—white cotton overalls, white latex gloves and white wellington boots. Worn white tiles separated by an off-white grout cover the floor, and the tile between my boots is cracked.

My body starts walking and the shock unbalances me, but I place one foot in front of the other without thinking. There is a single pair of footsteps ahead, someone in black boots, but I march in time with an unknown number behind.

I pass through a doorway into a corridor in which the dirty concrete floor curves up to meet plastered walls.

I smell blood. After thirty-two paces, at a drain hole clogged with hair, we turn right, and I lose count of my steps until we pass through a curtain of plastic strips which pull at my hood and drag over my shoulders. A number of doorways lead off either side. After twenty-two paces, I pass over a metal threshold and into a cold, brightly lit room. I walk over to a switch on the floor. As the footsteps behind march in different directions for different distances, I identify three distinct pairs. Someone walks around the room, pausing three times to plug-in something electrical, before coming up behind me and doing the same. They remove the hood and for a moment I am dazzled.

Rows of connected plastic trays, six inches by four, lie empty on a motionless conveyor belt. To the left, a tall hopper feeds a metallic chute, and to the right, the conveyor leads under a Perspex cover. Everything drips with water and there is a faint smell of rancid blood.

A heavy door slams shut.

A fragment of decaying meat is trapped in a roller of the conveyor belt.

A claxon sounds and machines all around whir simultaneously into life. From beneath the chute's metalwork, more vacuum-formed trays emerge and as I position myself to face the chute, I glimpse an analogue wall clock—it is fifteen minutes past twelve. Minced meat emerges down the chute. I press the floor switch with my right foot to operate a blade and portion the meat at two pounds. I'm not sure how I know it is two pounds, but it is, exactly. I catch it in my right hand, rotate to my right and place the meat in a tray. There is a small metallic disc in my palm. I press the switch again, take the portioned meat and place it in the tray alongside. Two more empties appear and I fill them with meat. As the next two appear, the first row disappears under the Perspex and a blast of gas adds to the cacophony. The smell of animal fat is everywhere.

I repeat the process.

I repeat it again.

And again and again.

Blood leaks out from the machinery and pools at my feet.

I glimpse the clock on every rotation. I've done four rows per minute for an hour, and this is not a dream— I've been in it too long. I have never worked in a factory. I had a life, but this wasn't it. I am trapped. It is my body, and I am in it, but it is not me. I want to scream, I want to cry, but I just pack meat, like a machine.

The nausea suddenly increases and I desperately need to gag, but just as I can stomach it no longer, a buzzer sounds and my machine stops. I resume my initial position, head bowed, as if in stand-by. Something plastic and heavy scrapes along the floor, accompanied by irregular, wellington-clad footsteps. There is a heaving of breath and a grunt, and the hopper rattles with the thump of a fresh new load. The footsteps pace away, the buzzer sounds twice and I resume my role.

An hour or so later, this happens again.

And again and again.

At a quarter to eight, I enter stand-by, but nothing is added to the hopper. Instead, the conveyer continues to feed the last row of packed meat through the machine, followed by rows of empties until the claxon sounds and everything stops. Someone walks up behind me, places a cover over my head, and disconnects an electrical socket. We all exit the room, four of us marching in time behind someone in black boots, take twenty-two paces to the plastic curtain, eight paces to the corner, and thirty-two paces down the corridor, where we turn right into the room in which we began.

At the cracked tile, I rotate a hundred and eighty degrees and lose consciousness.

My motions are controlled and my range of view is set. My life consists of waking up shortly before a quarter past twelve, walking to the brightly lit room and packing meat.

My fellow shift workers and I are always led there and back by someone in black boots, one of three people, who never speak. There are four production lines—one large, two mediums and one small. In every shift, I will pack three thousand six hundred large portions, four thousand eight hundred medium portions, or five thousand four hundred small portions. Every four shifts, I see exactly the same thing. My fellow workers, who I only glimpse from behind on the medium and small lines, are dressed like me. We occupy the same floor space and pack the same amount of meat in the same number of packets.

There is only one variable, the product. Mechanically recovered meat is piped into each mincer from below, but when it falls below standard the production line pauses for chainmail-clad hands to lift a blue plastic tray, and deposit extra-lean meat in the hopper. There are six distinct Grunts, they work in pairs and complete six shifts in a row. Their visits always coincide with an unbearable desire to vomit and I realise this is because I am somehow the monitor of the fat content, through the metallic disc in my palm.

The drone of the machines is punctuated by the slicing of blade and the jetting of gas. Out of rhythm are the sounds from the background. The slam of doors. The squeal of tyres. The slaughter of cows. Every shift, some will be dragged until their necks pop—it is a unique noise. Others will make it alive to later stages and the butchers cheer louder the longer the torture goes on.

The conveyor belt is black, the metalwork is silver, the walls and floor are white. The red puddles of blood are an inch deep when we leave. Two cleaners now always wait outside, with their mops and buckets, and are silent when we pass. They have black boots and white rubber trousers, and they shuffle inefficiently.

The lines move forward and we pack more meat.

Shift number one hundred and one. My nearest colleague, on the other medium line, falls onto their machine. All lines cease instantly, a red light flashes and the room claxon sounds continuously. I am flicked into stand-by, head down. Two pairs of black boots enter the room, bringing with them the smell of cigarettes. I don't know why I should know this smell, it has no relevance to packing meat. They rush over, slowing their pace as they arrive. The siren stops.

"Drunk on the job?" jokes the first. He has a West-country accent, unthreatening. "Oh no, the useless twat's caught his sleeve in the belt." He moves to my colleague's right, stiffens his legs and jerks backwards.

"Now what?" asks the second. He is West-country too, a bit higher pitched.

"Reboot the fucker," replies the first. His colleague kicks my fellow shift worker up the arse and they both guffaw as they leave. A moment later, my colleague crouches on the ground with their back towards me—I think he's a he, though I don't know why.

I think I'm a he, too.

My fellow shift worker pulses with a small shock and resumes his stand-by position, the claxon sounds and the lines power up.

He doesn't move.

The siren resumes, I switch into stand-by and the Black Boots return. They stand either side of him.

"Work, you lazy bastard!" shouts the deeper voiced.

His colleague sniggers. "What do you reckon?"

"See if a clip round the ear won't sort him."

The Black Boots to the left take a step away, his hips lean back and, out of sight, his upper body delivers a blow.

My fellow worker topples toward the machine, rotating as he falls rigidly to the floor. A surgical mask hides his face, but he has very pale skin and the most amazing blue eyes. They look right into me and I sense a gentle soul.

"At least the Poles would put up a fight," jokes the

higher pitched Black Boots.

"Well, I don't miss 'em," says the other. He flicks a switch on the machine. "Grab that foot," he says and they drag him away on his head.

The door clangs shut and the packing continues.

The next shift, someone wearing bigger white boots replaces him.

The production line never pauses for long—cows at one end, minced meat at the other. I've done one thousand shifts.

I leave the storeroom with a weight upon my back and white rucksack straps over my shoulders. Another pair of feet have joined our shift, and I am led to the end of the smalls' line. The new viewpoint disorientates me and I can't quite see the fifth worker, but I am saddened that it's not my blue-eyed colleague because they are too tall. Then I realise no-one has plugged me in to a power source.

I don't want to faint.

I don't want to fall over.

I don't want the attention of the Black Boots.

The claxon sounds, the conveyors begin and I take a roll of yellow special offer stickers from a box of many more. I unpeel a sticker and attach it lightly to my gloved first finger, then do the same with two more stickers on my second and third fingers. When a new row emerges from the machine I place them one at a time in the top right corner on the three furthest packets, before unpeeling a fourth sticker and attaching it to the nearest packet. I prepare three more stickers as the next row appears and repeat the process.

When the machine hisses with gas and seals the packet, it also places a label in the top left-hand corner. Once the empty packets have run through, the word 'error' is replaced by the details. I pack lean minced beef for the Great British Beef Company, which contains less than 20% fat, sells for fifty pounds an ounce and must be used by the 12th of January.

The shift ends with me having attached five thousand four hundred and fifty-two special offer stickers, as I wasted fifty-two on the empties.

I paused six times for the fat content to be improved.

At no stage was I plugged in to the mains.

For eight shifts, I've worn the white rucksack and stuck special offer stickers on the smalls' line. Each of the previous shifts required pauses to lean-up the supply, but I've done two thousand packets non-stop and my sticker placement is ever so slightly flawed—I'm approaching the edge of the packets.

They are less than a millimetre from the edge—I cannot control this.

They are at the edge—I cannot stop this.

They are creeping over the edge—I cannot save myself.

The alarm goes off, the four production lines cease and I switch into stand-by.

I know it's me. I know I've failed, but if the lines

would just restart it will be fine.

The door opens and I smell tobacco.

Two men approach from behind.

On top of the tobacco is stale sweat.

"Battery issue?" suggests the deeper voiced.

One of them opens the rucksack. "Fucked if I'd know," says the higher pitched and closes it again. "Reboot?" he asks

There's nothing I can do to brace myself.

I rock forward on being kicked.

They laugh as they walk away.

I crouch down and an electric shock pulses through my core, a deafening sensory overload as my circuits are purged. I stand up, dizzy and needing to vomit, which my body won't allow. The claxon sounds and I remember the meat, the production line and the special offer stickers, which I place correctly.

I still remember my blue-eyed colleague.

Our numbers are back down to four and I pack meat for five hundred and thirteen shifts before, once again, I'm given the rucksack and attach special offer stickers on the smalls' line. For many shifts now, the meat's consistency has been good and an unseen Grunt hasn't brought in additional red meat to lean-up the supply. My flawed placement of the stickers will mean a reboot, but it is the black booted humiliation, the risk of falling and the possibility of damage, that I fear.

The production line commences, I retrieve a sticker roll and concentrate my entire being into their placement.

A hundred rows exit the machine.

The sticker placement is perfect.

I am using my left hand.

I freeze—I'd used my right hand before.

The claxon sounds, the red light flashes and the machines cease. I go into stand-by.

The door opens, the smell of tobacco fills the air and the two Black Boots walk up behind me. The alarm subsides.

"That's weird," says the deeper voiced of the two. "There's fuck all wrong."

"Reboot?" asks high-pitched Black Boots.

"Worth a try," replies his colleague as he turns to go, then he shouts "No, don't—"

"Can't I have my bit of fun?"

"If you pay my share of the fine."

I don't get kicked and they leave the room. I crouch down, pulse with a shock and resume stand-by, only I'm not, I'm doing it instinctively, I'm faking.

The claxon sounds and the lines restart. Conscious effort is required and I grab the sticker roll, but as I remove the first sticker it attaches to my thumb and by the time I have it on my forefinger I should have placed three.

The siren goes off.

I fake stand-by.

I drop the sticker roll, which rolls across the floor.

The Black Boots return.

"What the fuck?" says the deeper voiced.

The other stands in front of me. "You fuckin' retard!" he shouts—his breath is putrid. "You wanna play silly fuckers?"

I stare at his boots, desperate not to flinch.

"Let's just take him to the engineer," says the other. He flicks a switch somewhere on the machine. "Get that shoulder."

The high-pitched Black Boots move closer and bends down to look up into my face. His is pudgy, and he has small eyes.

"Are you staring at me, you cunt?"

"Don't be daft," says his companion, who hooks a hand under my arm. "C'mon, it ain't worth the aggro,"

"I'm telling you—that fucker looked at me!" The high-pitched Black Boots hesitates, then grabs me by my armpit and I lose sensation in my hand. They drag me on my heels from the packing room.

We pass under the PVC curtain, around the corner, and beyond the storeroom. After another two corners, we stop and one of them knocks on a door.

A strip light flickers overhead.

They knock again.

"He's probably in the canteen. Coffee?" suggests the deeper voiced.

"Good idea—we can see if his mate's done the baccy run."

They prop me up against the doorframe, facing out and continue along the corridor.

The feeling in my hand returns.

A lorry arrives somewhere outside, and stops with a hiss of air brakes. A reversing siren beeps for a moment before the brakes hiss again and its diesel engine thrums slowly on tick-over.

I stop feigning stand-by and nearly fall over. I push myself upright against the door and walk further along the corridor, through another PVC curtain, into the open.

It is dark outside, and hot.

An articulated lorry is in the loading bay. Under spotlights at the rear, a man in a forklift loads pallets, while the lorry driver reads a paper in his cab. I run to the side of the trailer, but there is no access underneath. I keep close, inch forwards and jump up behind the cab. There is a small gap, under a noisy air-conditioning outlet, and I squeeze in.

It takes a long time to fill the lorry, though motion at the rear is constant. Finally, the rear doors are bolted shut, someone shouts an "Okay," to the driver and bangs the side, twice. A moment later, we're on the move.

I shuffle my feet rapidly to remain hidden as we make a tight, right turn and the trailer tyres squeal loudly. The lorry straightens, makes a gentler left turn and comes to a stop with a hiss. The driver lowers his window. A few muffled words are shared with a female, some paperwork is stamped and we exit the factory gates.

A poorly lit industrial unit flashes past too closely to make out any details. We come to a junction and pull out onto a wider road, into a residential area, where the stink of rotting garbage fills the air. Increasing numbers of shopfronts, all boarded-up, suggests we are heading into town.

We stop and I risk a glimpse up the road. We're at traffic lights and signs state we're on the ring road, in the left-hand lane, for the motorway. The lights change to green. The driver presses the throttle and the lorry pitches forward, building vibrations to a resonant frequency that bounces me out of position. I leap to avoid falling and land awkwardly in the gutter.

I test my limbs. My right hip is seized and I have no control over the leg, but there is no pain. I roll over to an empty shopfront and haul myself up with the drainpipe. My reflection startles me, as I'm still wearing the facemask.

I try to take off my gloves, but they extend too far up my sleeves, so I remove the facemask and look up.

I have a white latex face.

The individual features are familiar, but not the whole.

I stare into my grey eyes, into the abyss.

I have a family—no, I had a family. I cannot recall their faces. I cannot recall their names.

The sky has lightened from the east and my batteries are fading. A white van with 'MEAT' on the side speeds past. If I had a breath to hold, I would.

Further along the road is a cemetery, overgrown and forgotten. I will crawl through the trash, I will find a place to hide, and I will die again. I pray to God that this time I will rest in peace.

JAY MILLINGTON

Jay Millington, a university lecturer in fluid dynamics, recently enjoyed a student's perspective to complete an MA in Creative Writing at Bath Spa. He worked on a comic, metafictional thriller about academia, paranoia and circumstantial evidence. It's nearly finished, but he keeps getting distracted by short stories.

He's read these at various events, with topics ranging from one man's journey across time and space in search of the perfect toothpaste, to losing his detachable penis, 300 words that helped the NBW team into a flash-slam final. Luckily, after dying on stage for a postmodern piece at a graveyard, he made a full recovery, unless he's been brought back to life as a cyborg...

Find out more at <u>about.me/jaymillington</u>

All The Moor Remembers

Chloe Headdon

It had been a month since he'd buried his father.

Guy drove up onto the moor, in and out of thick banks of fog that coalesced suddenly out of the darkness like gathering wraiths, smothering the dry-stone walls, the thorny trees, the narrow, winding road. He tried full-beam headlights but that only made the problem worse, the wisps becoming a blank white mass into which his car plunged, headlong. He finally settled on half-beams, keeping his speed under 30mph, every shred of his attention fixed on the few feet he could see of the road, appearing and vanishing under his car like an enormous treadmill. For long stretches it felt like he wasn't moving at all. At other times the thought of missing a turn or crashing into something rose up in Guy like a fever, making his eyes strain harder, his knuckles turn white as he clutched the wheel.

Then the fog would clear and he'd relax again, spotting familiar landmarks: a twisted thorn, a huddled mass of boulders.

This was still the Dartmoor he knew. It was just the fog making him jumpy.

At least when he was focused on driving, he could briefly forget his destination. The rest of the time doubts circled in his mind like birds. What would it be like at home? Better—it had to be better. It certainly couldn't get any worse. Guy remembered the last time he'd made this journey to Withywell-in-the-Moor, dressed in his best black suit, going over and over his father's eulogy in his head. Not because he thought he might forget it, but because he'd been afraid his true feelings might glare through. Tone was just as important as the words themselves. So he'd practised and practised, and though he wasn't much of a public speaker, he'd somehow managed to pull it off at the funeral.

One final ordeal, the lies of love and gratitude like ashes in his mouth. But at least that had been the end of it.

Now Guy hoped for a new beginning.

Fog rolled over his car again. Guy scowled as the temperature plummeted further; it was already a freezing November night, and the car's heating was on the blink. Groping for the controls, he accidentally brushed the wrong button. A burst of static squawked from the radio. Guy jerked and risked a quick glance across to correct the mistake. He brought his eyes back—

And saw a shape materialise right in front of him: tall, dark, thin. A person.

There was a person standing in the middle of the road.

Guy yelled, stamping hard on the brake and yanking the wheel sideways. The car skidded, tyres screeching, but it was still travelling forwards at speed. For a moment everything was noise and panic and the careening knowledge that a human being was about to crash over his bonnet, he was going to hurt someone, kill them possibly. He had no chance. They had no chance.

There was no impact.

The next thing Guy felt was a series of rattling bumps as the rear wheels hit grass, then a hard lurch backwards as the car dropped down into a shallow ditch. It came to rest facing the road, headlights angled slightly upwards, illuminating a white wall of fog. The engine stalled. Warning lights on the dashboard glared red.

"Shit."

Guy couldn't move. His heart was racing. He felt like he'd left his stomach somewhere on the tarmac. Then the thought of the pedestrian overcame his shock and his hands flew, shaking, to the seatbelt release.

"Shit, shit, shit."

He fought his way out of the car, shoving the door wildly when it dug into the peaty earth. Tussocks of grass threatened to trip him as he stumbled up onto the road.

"I'm sorry, I'm so sorry! Are you all right?"

No voice answered his call. Guy's own voice sounded oddly muted, like a radio slightly out of tune. He sucked in a few breaths, cold air searing his lungs.

"Are you all right? Hello?"

Silence.

The person must have jumped aside just in time. Were they lying hurt somewhere, invisible in the fog? Maybe they were even stunned from the fall. Guy held his breath, ears straining for any tell-tale sound: a groan, a whimper. But silence reigned as though a thick blanket muffled all noise, and at last he had to gasp again, heart hammering.

Guy fumbled his smartphone from his pocket and switched on the torch setting. "Where are you?" he shouted. "Make a noise! Please, just let me know you're okay..."

He began to work his way back up the road, searching from side to side. The torch wasn't any better than the full-beams; if he tried to shine it directly ahead, it just painted a flat white spot on the fog. He focused on the ground, nerves winding tighter and tighter as he waited for the light to fall upon someone.

"Where are you?"

But everywhere he looked, the road was empty. Guy extended his search, venturing deep onto the grass on either side, staggering over the rough ground. At one point he saw something rise up before him, tall and dark, and his heart faltered; but it was only one of the standing stones that dotted Dartmoor, a lonely grey monolith. It also couldn't have been what he'd seen, since it was a good ten feet off the road. Guy stared at it for a long moment in confusion, then on he went. What the hell was going on? If someone had nearly hit *him* with their car, he'd be screaming blue murder, not hiding in the fog like a child playing games...

"Who's there? Anyone?"

Guy's nerves were beginning to loosen, doubt creeping in. He tried to recall what he'd seen. Could he have mistaken a break in the fog for a solid shape? It was possible, but on the other hand, it had looked defined, contoured, like a body. He trudged back to the middle of the road and spun in a slow circle.

"Is—someone—THERE?"

Guy's desperate shout went unanswered, and with that he finally accepted the truth: there was no one else here. There had never been anyone here. He'd been tricked by tiredness, paranoia, and the damn fog. Relief and frustration warred within him as he turned towards the bright white haloes cast by his car's headlights.

The car itself didn't seem damaged, and the engine grumbled back into life when Guy turned the ignition. But it was stuck. Trying to coax it back onto the road just resulted in the back wheels spinning uselessly in the ditch, digging deeper and deeper, until Guy gave up. He checked his phone. No signal.

"All right," he muttered. "Guess I'm walking home."

Guy woke groggily in his childhood bedroom. Cold sweat glued his t-shirt and shorts to his skin, and for a moment his sense of time collapsed, past shunting forwards into present. He was twelve years old again, waking, screaming, in this bed after a nightmare. If he opened his eyes, he'd see his parents silhouetted in the doorway, stark against the soft glow of the corridor. He'd see his mum start forwards, reaching for him anxiously, see his father put a firm hand on her shoulder. He'd see her stop.

Guy opened his eyes. He looked.

The door was closed, the room dim, and a flood of shame hit him then for how easily he'd fallen back into old memories. But shame was mixed with anger, too. Richard Horrox had never been one to comfort, or 'coddle' as he'd called it. Guy remembered how his father had sent his mum back to bed that night and stepped into the room himself, looming above Guy's bed, a great black shape. He remembered his father's words spoken through the darkness, flat with disappointment:

"You had another one."

"Yes. I'm sorry."

"Guy, you know why you keep getting nightmares, don't you? We've spoken about this."

"Because I'm not being brave," Guy whispered.

"That's right." His father leaned closer, so that his breath touched Guy's face. *"The nightmares feed off your fear, Guy. As long as you're scared to have them, they'll never go away. You have to show them you're not weak. The more scared you are, the worse it will be for you."*

"I'm sorry," Guy said again. *"I'm trying."*

"Are you?"

Guy scrubbed his hands over his face. "Bastard," he muttered. He shoved away the clammy bedsheets and went to take a shower.

He walked into the kitchen ten minutes later, fully dressed. His mum, Joyce, was already sat at the table, scraping butter over toast, a newspaper spread on the chequered tablecloth.

"What are you going to do about your car, then?"

Guy suppressed a sigh. Obviously they were going to continue the conversation they'd started at eleven o'clock the night before, when he'd quietly let himself into the house—frozen through, exhausted from the walk—to find his mum waiting up for him in a fluffy pink dressing gown. She'd been upset that Guy hadn't called, but at least her anger had been offset by relief that he was finally home and safe. Now, from the rough way she was treating her toast, Guy guessed his period of grace was over.

"Morning Mum." He tentatively kissed her cheek. "I told you, I'll call Tom. Hopefully he can tow it out."

"And what then? What if you've damaged your car? Tom's a very kind man but he can't spend hours towing you to the nearest garage, wherever that is."

"The car's fine, Mum. It started last night, I just couldn't get it onto the road."

"You don't know that it's fine. You drove it into a *ditch*, for heaven's sake!"

"It was an accident."

He knew he'd chosen his words poorly when her eyes narrowed. She placed her knife down with a clang.

"An accident? There's no such thing as a car *accident*, Guy! Haven't I warned you about bombing round like you do? Well, you're going to have to figure out what to tell everyone, because I'm certainly not admitting my son was driving dangerously!"

"We don't have to tell anyone anything. It's none of their business," Guy said, more calmly than he felt. "Look,"—he reached for the kitchen phone—"I'll call Tom now, we can go right out and—"

"You're not going *now*, are you?"

Guy paused, thumb hovering over the buttons. "I need to get my car back."

"We're going to the churchyard this morning. Don't you remember? When we spoke on the phone, we said we'd go lay flowers on Dad's grave. Please, love," his mum said, seeing his wary expression. "You haven't visited him since the funeral."

"Mum, I told you, things have been really busy at the paper. Why don't we go this afternoon?"

"I've having tea with Philippa this afternoon, and I can't let her down, not after she's been so kind. Please, Guy. I don't want to go on my own."

Guy still hesitated. He itched to get his car back as soon as possible, but his mum was looking at him with such fragile need, and he suddenly realised he'd been cruel, leaving her alone for a whole month. If he wanted things to be better between them, maybe he had to make the first move—however much he wished it was the other way around.

He put the phone down.

Guy walked with his mum towards the heart of Withywell-in-the-Moor, past dozens of little stone cottages. The church lay on one side of the main square, the other edges occupied by a medieval tithe barn, and a quaint, ivy-clad pub. All very picturesque, not to mention popular with the tourists that flocked to the village every summer.

Guy had never liked the place. Maybe it was the ubiquitous grey stone that gave the buildings a drab, cold air even in the brightest sunshine, as though nothing could warm them. Maybe it was the skulking presence of the moor all around, mile upon mile of wilderness encircling the valley.

Maybe it was the lack of escape, both now and in his childhood.

To add to his resentment, the short stroll took much longer than usual. Withywell's residents were all out and about, making the most of a sunny morning, and everyone was determined to speak to his mum.

"How are you doing, Joyce, my love?"

"It was a beautiful funeral..."

"You know Richard will always be in our hearts."

"So many people—we had to stand at the back of the church!"

"A heart attack... I still can't believe it."

Guy stood stiffly, his mum gripping one arm, a wicker basket of flowers tucked under his other. It was all the same stuff he'd heard at the funeral, the same bland condolences, and from all the same people. When would it stop? His mum, though, seemed happy to receive so much attention; wearing a sombre dress, she thanked everyone for their kindness, let them hold her hand, smiled bravely. Few people spoke to Guy, mistaking his silence for grief, but he was glad of that. He didn't trust himself to speak.

At long last they passed under the roofed lychgate into the churchyard. St Peter's was large for a parish church, its tall, dark granite tower stabbing at the sky. The churchyard itself was bounded by a low stone wall and hunched yew trees, the grass between the graves short and tough. Many of the oldest headstones held the names of farms alongside the names of the dead, just visible on their pitted, lichen-dappled surfaces. Generations of families lay side by side.

His father's resting place was among the newer plots, at the furthest distance from the church. The headstone, new and clean, had a slightly unreal look, like a prop in a film. When Guy didn't show any sign of placing the flowers down, his mum took them, touching the headstone lovingly.

"Hello sweetheart. Look who's come to see you," she said, and started crying.

How long they stood there, Guy didn't know. Minutes felt like hours as he tried to maintain an appropriately sad expression, hugging his mum around the shoulders; he didn't dare risk checking his watch. More frustrating still was the knowledge that Richard would probably *enjoy* his son's discomfort...

No, Guy told himself sternly. Don't think like that. He doesn't know or feel anything.

The thought gave him a furtive little thrill.

People left them alone in the churchyard out of respect. But the moment they stepped back through the lychgate, well-wishers found them again like pests attracted by the scent of grief. Guy fixed a smile on his face, listened politely, shook various neighbours' hands. The fourth time their walk home was interrupted, he was starting to develop an unpleasant notion. By the fifth, he knew he was right:

This was what it was going to be like from now on. This was why he had to stay away from Withywell as much as possible.

Guy had imagined his father's untimely death would give him release, freedom... *something*. The dark pall of Richard's presence should have been lifted from here.

But what he hadn't counted on was his father's legacy. These people hadn't known the bully Richard became behind closed doors, and now they never would, because Guy could never tell them. He couldn't take back those words he'd said at the funeral.

Well played, Dad, Guy thought bitterly as he clasped another neighbour's hand.

The *Cat and Fiddle* was busy that evening, a wash of warm, stale air and voices hitting Guy as he slipped through the side entrance. He'd originally intended to avoid the pub, but after a difficult afternoon, he needed a drink almost as much as he needed to escape the house.

First, his car had refused to start. After much pleading with the engine and—when that failed—swearing, Guy had grudgingly asked his neighbour to tow it to a garage, where a mechanic grunted something about "getting parts in". Guy had then returned home to suffer his mum's remarks, including her friend Philippa's thoughts on his 'accident'. Things had finally come to a head at dinner, when, sick of seeing his father's belongings strewn around the house as though nothing had happened, Guy had dared to suggest they start to sort through them. Big mistake. His mum's wail still rang in his ears as he made for the quieter end of the bar:

"I don't understand you, Guy! Your dad's gone, do you want to get rid of what's left of him, too?"

Wouldn't that be nice, Guy thought, ordering a beer.

He grabbed a table in one of the pub's shadowed nooks,

from where he could watch the crowd surreptitiously. The *Cat and Fiddle*'s regulars were just as he remembered; Guy wondered if some of them ever aged. There was Jim Evans in his faded flannel shirt, and of course Mick Cartwright, red-faced and portly as ever, holding court from the exact same barstool he'd occupied for the past however-many years. Mick gestured expansively with his pint—third or fourth, to go by the deep flush of his cheeks—while his audience grinned and laughed.

"Glowing red eyes, she said. Like the Devil 'imself!"

"Hooves as well, was it?" asked Jim.

"Ah, no. No, no." Mick smiled knowingly and shook his head. "Not hooves. *Wings.*"

"Fuck's sake!" declared Jim, tossing a few crisps into his labrador's snapping mouth.

Liz Whiddon came over and slid onto a stool, delicately sipping her spritzer. "Who's this, Mick?"

"Julia Abbott, up at Stonecross Farm. Mad old bat."

"Oh." Liz's face fell slightly. "Poor dear."

Jim snorted. "You ask me, she's never been right, even before her husband—" He clenched a fist and yanked it up beside his face.

"Guy? Guy! Thought I spotted you hiding over here!"

Guy looked up, nearly choking on his beer. Liz's husband Ian was looming at him around the corner, grinning with more enthusiasm than Guy thought his presence deserved.

"Oh. Hi."

"How are things? Still with the local rag down in Plymouth?"

"Yeah. Just back to visit Mum for the weekend."

The mention of a parent was enough to dampen the smile on Ian's face. Guy's heart plummeted.

"Listen, that was a terrible business with your dad, really terrible. We all miss him. Hang on," Ian said, brightening again as he spotted Guy's half-empty glass, "let me get you another. We'll toast his memory, eh?"

"No," Guy said, "thanks, but I really ought to—"

Ian was already heading towards the bar, calling and waving for everyone's attention. Mick and his cohort looked over, drinks half-raised to mouths.

Guy left the pub a few hours later, various well-worn anecdotes about Richard ringing through his head while as many pints of best Devon bitter sloshed around his stomach. Funny, he thought, how each toast had become easier than the last. By the end his smile had felt almost natural.

Outside, fog was gathering again, subtle in the darkness. Guy remembered his car and glared at the wisps, drunkenly seeing malice in the way they shrouded the main square, curled around buildings, haunted the churchyard beyond. Someone was in the church; yellow light filled the arched windows, though that glow was already becoming dim and murky. Above, he could still make out the Gothic tower if he squinted, a different kind of blackness rising against the sky, its pinnacles like horns.

A dog started barking, jolting Guy out of his reverie. He turned to head home—

And froze as he spotted the person beneath the lychgate: tall, featureless, silhouetted between the pillars. Had they been there a moment ago? He didn't remember seeing them, but he wasn't exactly sober. Guy stared. Perhaps it was his imagination, but from the still, silent way the figure was standing, he got the prickling sense they were watching him. He took a step forwards for a better look, forgot the curb, and half-tripped from the pub's doorstep into the road.

When he looked up again, the figure was gone.

Guy blinked hard. "No you don't," he muttered, slurring. "Not this time..."

He strode across the square, the cheery sounds of the pub fading behind him. At the gate he paused, hand gripping the metal ring, so cold it burned his skin. He couldn't see anyone in the churchyard. Guy's head swum; he swiped at his eyes, which were having trouble focusing. Wasn't he meant to be going home?

The gate's hinges squealed as he opened it.

"Where are you? Where the fuck are you?"

Guy struck a path across the grass, peering around. If he'd been scared the previous night, now drink filled him with bravado as he searched among the graves. The person in the road might have vanished, but he wouldn't be fooled again.

Back and forth he went, occasionally bumping into headstones that lurched unexpectedly out of the darkness, turning back on himself whenever he met the boundary wall. Everything smelled of damp earth and mildew. He called out a few times, but the fog seemed to swallow his voice, and in any case, there was no reply.

His hands and face were numb and beaded with moisture, a wet chill penetrating his clothes, when he realised the lights in the church had gone out. The fog had closed in so much that he couldn't even see the building anymore, though he knew it must be close. Guy cast around, trying to find his bearings. Where was the gate? He couldn't tell, all he could see were graves. Even the weak, distant light from the pub had somehow vanished, darkness surrounding the churchyard.

It was also then, standing lost and alone, that he noticed it: the silence. The dog had stopped barking, and everywhere silence pressed on him like a weight.

Something passed him in the night.

Guy heard a soft, rushing sound, felt a disturbance in the air. He cried out and spun, nearly losing his balance.

"*Shit*! Who's that?"

It passed him again on the other side.

"Who's there? What you playin' at?"

He waited, heart racing, fists raised, but—nothing. No noise, no sense of anyone near him. Though, Guy thought fuzzily, it hadn't felt much like a *person*. It had been lighter, swifter than that... A bird? There was something about the sound that had reminded him of wings...

He'd had enough—phantom person be damned. Guy lurched in what he desperately hoped was the right direction. After a minute his foot dropped blindly from the grass down onto gravel, and his stomach flipped. He veered along the path, going faster now, footsteps crunching loudly in the silence—

And stopped dead as the dark, closed doors of St Peter's formed in front of him.

"Shit," Guy said again. He'd followed the path the wrong way.

He turned back. He was nearly running for the gate when some primal instinct warned him: a breath of air against the back of his neck, a sense of something bearing down from behind, fast, near-silent. Guy gasped. He went to throw himself down, but with his head spinning, the ground seemed to fly up to hit him instead. Air exploded from his lungs; gravel bit savagely into his cheek and palms.

Something huge swooped over him, low enough that he felt a faint brush along his back—softly yielding, like feathers. Terror swamped him, but revulsion too, that silky touch somehow worse than the impact he'd expected. Guy gave a muffled yell. Then it passed over him, vanishing into the night, and he forced himself to stagger back to his feet, swallowing down his nausea.

Out. He had to get out.

He was within sight of the gate's ghostly form when the fog swirled and parted. A black shape crossed the path in front of him: there then gone, moving with astonishing speed. Guy changed course, plunging back among the graves. Screw the gate; he'd vault the stone wall if he had to! For a few seconds he thought his gambit had worked as he tore wildly around graves, no sign of pursuit—

A screech filled the night, like no sound Guy had ever heard: high, eldritch, somewhere between a peregrine's scream and the squeal of rusty metal. It pierced him like a blade of ice, stealing the courage from his heart and strength from his legs. He fell hard. His temple clipped something solid, pain exploding through his head.

The shriek grew louder. Whatever made it was closing

fast. Guy tensed and wrapped his arms around his head to protect himself, but all he felt was a sharp blast of air. The sound moved away—straight up, towards the sky, fading quickly. Before it vanished altogether it started to break, stuttering, and in his pain, fear, and drink-addled confusion, Guy thought it sounded almost like...

Laughter.

Guy lost track of time as he lay there. But at last he found the strength to roll over, peering blearily at the pale shape to his left: a marble headstone. He was on top of a grave. Through the darkness he could read the words, black against the white, crisply carved:

RICHARD ANTHONY HORROX
1949 – 2017
Death has been swallowed up in victory

Between the hangover and the throbbing pain from smacking his head, it took Guy a while the next morning to remember. When he did, he lurched upright in his narrow bed, the room spinning then settling around him.

Wings? Something about wings.

He ate breakfast with his mum, trying to ignore the way her eyes lingered disapprovingly on the bruised lump on his temple. She said nothing but Guy sensed another lecture brewing, presumably on the subject of drinking too much. He was oddly grateful for the silence; it gave him the opportunity to think. By the time he finished his tea and cornflakes, most of the conversation in the pub had come back to him. He got up and grabbed his mum's keys from the bowl.

"Need to borrow the car, won't be long."

"What? You're not *driving*? You might have concussion!"

"I'm fine, Mum. See you later."

Her protests pursued him to the front door. As Guy grabbed his coat, he spotted his reflection in the mirror hanging beside the peg: the bruise was worse than he'd thought, a stark, vivid purple against his pale skin. He hastily raked his dark hair down over his forehead and left the house.

True to his memory, Stonecross Farm lay in the next valley over, the home farm tucked away from the windswept reach of the high moor. An old stone farmhouse was surrounded by more modern barns and outbuildings. As Guy pulled up in the yard, he saw a wiry woman in her late sixties unloading sacks from the back of an ancient green Land Rover. Her face, creased and weathered like Dartmoor stone, was vaguely familiar. Despite the cold, she'd pushed the sleeves of her muddy jacket up to the elbow. She slammed the tailgate and watched Guy warily as he got out of the car.

"Can I help you?"

"Julia Abbott?" he called.

"Yes."

"I'm so sorry to trouble you," Guy said, coming over. "You don't know me, but I'm—

"I know who you are. You're Richard Horrox's son."

Guy paused—surprised not just at being cut off, but also at the way she said his father's name. People usually mentioned Richard with more warmth than that. "Oh, yes. I am. Guy," he stammered. A flash of inspiration struck him then, and he fumbled his work lanyard from his coat pocket, showing her the plastic ID card. "I work for the *Plymouth Gazette*. I'm a reporter," he said, which was half true. He worked in the advertising department, but the card didn't specify that. Warming to the lie, he continued, "I'm working on a piece about local legends, and I heard down in Withywell that you believe you saw something? A creature?"

"Believe? There's no doubting what I saw, Mr Horrox. Plain as day." She gave the card a cursory glance, then sighed shortly. "Well your timing's not great, I'm just heading out to check on the cows. Unless you don't mind coming along, that is," she added dryly.

"No, that would be great. Thank you!"

Julia blinked in surprise, then jerked a thumb at the Land Rover. "Right. Better hop in, then."

They rattled along narrow, hedge-bound roads, the valley's patchwork of small fields and barren woodland vanishing as they climbed. Erupting onto the high moor, the horizon yawned wide before them, Dartmoor's bleak beauty hitting Guy like a slap. Craggy granite tors rose like thrones among the wilderness, burnished by the sun. Despite the bright day, the moor's colours were muted, a bleached palette of green, brown and grey, with thick clumps of gorse so dark they were nearly black. Guy shivered in the wind gusting though the Land Rover's open windows. To his frustration, the noise prevented them from speaking as they hurtled along, the road winding like a grey ribbon between the peaks.

Julia kept belted Galloways, black with a white belt around their middles. As the animals came into view, grazing placidly between stunted bushes and trees, she veered the Land Rover onto the grass and braked. The abrupt stop nearly shunted Guy into the dashboard. She hopped out and strode briskly towards the herd, Guy rushing to catch up, his long black coat flapping behind him.

"So, Mrs Abbott..."

"Don't call me that. It's Julia."

"Julia," he amended. "I was wondering—"

"Who told you, Mr Horrox?"

"Told me?"

"Who was talking about me in Withywell? Was it Mick Cartwright? I bet it was, drunken old fart..."

"Um," Guy mumbled, "I'm afraid I can't reveal my sources."

Julia snorted. "If you say so. My own damn fault, really. Shouldn't have said anything. I just thought it might be a good idea to warn people."

Guy half-tripped over a clump of grass. "Warn them?"

"I'm not the first to see strange things up here. My family have farmed the moor for a long, long time. My grandpa swore blind that he'd seen a ghost of a little boy playing in a ruined cottage one day. Now, he liked to tell tales, my gramps, but my grandma told me once that she'd seen a demon with red eyes—and her I *do* believe. Fiercest woman I ever knew! She said she saw it, and not three days later the roof of the local church collapsed, killing half the folk inside. Maybe it was coincidence, but Grandma always believed what she saw that day was an omen, a sign that death was coming, and she wasn't often wrong in my experience. And I'll tell you something: when I saw that creature fly over me, big as a man, with red eyes just like Grandma described, I felt it too. I felt like evil was staring down at me."

"Evil," Guy repeated numbly. "But, Mrs Abbott—Julia. What you described can't exist. Are you *certain* it wasn't an owl or a bird?"

"I've spent my whole life here. D'you think I'd get spooked by a bloody owl? No, listen." She tucked her hands into her pockets and turned to face him, wisps of grey hair flying in the breeze. "Maybe you'll think I'm talking nonsense, but since you've bothered coming over here, I'll say my piece if it's all the same. When you've spent as long on the moor as I have, you come to understand something. The people who've lived here... they leave a trace."

Guy thought of St Peter's, the rows and rows of headstones. "You mean like graves?"

"Yes, that. But I'm talking about something else, like a spirit or, I don't know, a feeling. It's always seemed to me that this land soaks up memories like water. I guess what I'm really trying to say, Mr Horrox, is... the moor *remembers*."

"I'm sorry,"—Guy shook his head helplessly—"I don't understand. Are you saying you think the creature was some kind of... ghost?"

Julia's mouth twisted. "I don't know what to call it exactly. But the land here is full of history. Hell, it's fit to bursting with it. And... well. I wouldn't be surprised if, once in a while, the moor gives something back."

She frowned away for a moment, crow's feet deepening around her blue eyes. Then a snort alerted her that the cows were advancing from behind, breath steaming in the air, and Julia came back to herself with a grin. "Sneak up all you like, I haven't got anything for you!" she told the animals, flapping a hand at them. "Silly things..." She glanced at Guy and the flash of good humour faded, wariness creeping back in. "Why are you so interested, Mr Horrox?"

"It's Guy. And like I said, I'm writing a piece—a column—about Dartmoor legends. My boss thought I was the best person for the job, growing up here."

"H'mm. You must be very committed to your work, to chase down a story at the weekend. Must have a good memory, too, if you don't need to make notes." She threw a pointed glance at Guy's empty hands.

Guy shoved them self-consciously into his pockets. "I, uh, forgot my notepad. Could I ask a few more questions, if that's all right? When did you see the creature?"

"Two, three weeks ago. No, it was three, I remember now. I was coming home from dinner with a friend."

"It was dark, then?"

"Don't sound so hopeful. It was *getting* dark. And I told you, I know what I saw."

"And where did you see it, exactly?"

"Heard it first. Bloody awful shriek, like nails down a chalkboard. Then it flew right over me. I was standing in the farmyard, you've seen the place."

"Right. Okay. Thank you." Guy nodded and frowned down at his trainers. Alcohol clouded his memory of the churchyard, impenetrable as fog, but he remembered that unearthly screech well enough; the mere thought of it sent tendrils of ice creeping through his veins. He had a feeling he'd remember it until the day he died.

Realising Julia had gone oddly silent, he dragged his gaze up again. She was watching him with a strange, intense look on her face—half suspicion, half curiosity, as though she couldn't quite decide something.

"What is it?" he asked.

"You don't know me, do you?" she said slowly. "Your father never mentioned me?"

Again Guy thought she seemed familiar, but he couldn't place her. "I'm sorry, no. Should he have?"

Julia made a noise in her throat, somewhere between a grunt and a mirthless laugh. After another moment's scrutiny, she drew a deep breath and folded her arms. "All right, might as well tell you, God help me. I'm not one to ignore a sign when I see it... Years back, my husband was involved in a hit and run outside the farm. Smashed his leg in three places. Driver didn't stop, didn't even slow, but Geoff recognised the car. Thing is, Mr Horrox, there are no cameras out here. No witnesses. It would have been our word against the driver's if we'd reported it, and Geoff didn't want to, bloody stubborn man. He just wanted to get back to work.

"But even when his leg healed, the pain didn't go away. Doctors couldn't explain it. Kept telling us it was *all in his head*. Geoff struggled on as best as he could, but it hurt his pride, not being able to do his fair share anymore. Proud man, my husband. And we couldn't afford to hire on help, not when we'd already thrown money at fancy private doctors to sit and scratch their heads. Eventually Geoff'd had enough. Sometimes I think the life insurance played a part, too. Certainly helped to keep the farm running, once he'd gone."

Guy stared, remembering Jim Evans down the pub, yanking a fist up over his head. As though he held a noose.

"I was there, at your dad's funeral," Julia added flatly. "Still not sure why I went. *Morbid interest*, I suppose. But I'll tell you something: Richard didn't deserve that lovely speech you gave him."

Guy still didn't know what to say. His heart was galloping, blood roaring in his ears. He felt sick.

"No," he said at last, knowing how horribly inadequate that sounded. Knowing he should offer some apology, even though it wasn't his to give.

Julia seemed to read his thoughts, because she offered him a smile then, a smile that was tired and grim, but not entirely without warmth either. "You want my advice, lad, you forget that man ever existed. You're better off without him."

"And what if I can't?" Guy found himself asking. He hated the way his voice emerged: small and weak, like a child's.

"Maybe not 'forget', then. But the past's the past— can't change it or make it go away. All you or I *can* do is make peace with what's gone. We don't do that, we might as well live in the past and not the present. Don't you think, Guy?"

He didn't answer.

* * *

Returning home was almost unbearable, but Guy had little choice. He spent the rest of the day moving restlessly around the house, trying to distract himself—difficult when Richard's belongings goaded him wherever he turned. His head felt like it was splitting open. Nausea rose and ebbed in him like a tide. Should he tell his mum? No, there was no point. She wouldn't believe him; she'd probably scream the house down. He needed to let it go, along with everything else.

A new start.

Just like he'd promised himself.

As dusk began to fall, Guy went into the garage in search of a proper torch. Rooting around on the workbench, cluttered with his father's tools, Guy's eye was caught by a hammer. It felt good in his hand: heavy, solid. Comforting. He tucked it into his belt.

Returning to the house, he bumped into his mum peeling potatoes in the kitchen. She stopped as she noticed the torch.

"You're not going to the pub again, are you?"

"No. Just need to pop out for a bit."

"Guy, can't it wait? I feel like I've barely seen you this weekend!"

Guy avoided her pleading look. "There's just one thing I need to do, Mum, it won't take long," he promised. "And we still have time. My car's in the garage, remember?"

He left before she could change his mind.

The last blush of sunset was gilding the high ground when he reached St Peter's, but deep in the valley, night had already begun to settle. Guy paused at the lychgate, torch off, letting his eyes adjust to the gloom. The churchyard was empty of all but the dead, the church's windows dark and blank.

He was alone.

He crossed the churchyard and took up position on the far side, where an old yew tree grew close to the wall, creating a nook into which he could tuck himself, crouching down. Guy gripped the torch tightly. It was time to prove Julia Abbott had seen nothing more than an owl; then, he told himself, he could move on.

The temperature dropped rapidly as he waited. Guy soon lost the feeling in his feet, cold seeping up from the earth through his thin-soled trainers. But he stayed where he was, eyes fixed on the murky churchyard. Though there was no fog tonight, visibility was still poor, the moon a thin crescent like a fingernail. The churchyard backed onto fields behind him, so the only real light came from the pub and houses across the square, just strong enough to outline the lychgate and the far wall.

Half an hour passed. Then an hour. The yew's fissured bark started to dig into Guy's flank. He was about to shift to a more comfortable position when he heard something: a faint *whumph* of air, high above, like a wingbeat. Guy looked up, past the thick canopy that was nearly indistinguishable from the darkness all around. He saw nothing. Not even stars.

Whumph.

Again. Closer.

Guy rested his thumb on the torch's switch. He straightened slowly, joints stiff with cold, then stepped out from the shelter of the tree.

He felt very exposed as he stalked among the graves. Even with his footsteps muffled by the grass, he feared his breathing would give him away, short and ragged. Would his plan work? He'd imagined feeling like a hunter, strong and fearless. In truth, he felt more like... bait. He turned down a line of headstones and saw the pale, familiar gleam of marble ahead.

Something passed him in the night.

Guy was ready this time. He flicked the torch's switch and swung the beam of light after the creature, catching a glimpse of a large, black shape swooping away. Then it banked sharply in the air and was gone. Shining the torch from side to side only showed him graves, the names of their occupants like a silent chorus.

Guy shivered, considering his next move. His quarry was too fast to spot mid-air. He'd have to find it when it landed instead...

He headed in the direction the creature had flown, vigilant in case it swooped down on him again. As he walked he scanned everything that could be considered a perch: tops of headstones, the boundary wall, even summoning the courage to venture under the canopies of the other yew trees. Nothing. He made a full circuit of the church itself, pointing the beam of light upwards, but it was too weak to reach the roofline, let alone the top of the high tower. If the creature was up there, he couldn't see it. Despite the bitter cold, Guy's skin was crawling as he came back to the main path. If anything, he felt like *he* was the one being watched...

A high, piercing shriek sounded from nearby. Guy whirled, torch aimed towards the back of the churchyard.

But there was nothing there. A moment later, the light stuttered, flashes like Morse code punctuating the darkness—

Before it died.

"No!"

Guy flicked the switch up and down, hopefully at first, then in increasing panic as the torch failed to turn back on.

"No, don't do this, come on... *Come on...*"

He was still preoccupied, berating himself for not changing the batteries, when he felt a breath caress the back of his neck. He froze. In the silence he heard a noise right behind him, a faint crunch, like feet shifting on gravel.

The torch clattered to the ground. Whatever was behind Guy didn't move, didn't make another sound, but he felt malice pouring off it like waves of frigid air. Evil, he thought, and the certainty struck an awful chord in his heart. *Evil.* He pulled the hammer from his belt, struggling to grip it in a hand turned suddenly numb.

There was a low chuckle.

"Scared, Guy?"

Guy's courage almost failed at that voice, like something from his nightmares. It was guttural, broken, almost unrecognisable as a voice at all, but that wasn't what terrified him. It wasn't even the fact that the creature knew his name.

It was the *way* it said it.

He tightened his hold on the hammer. "It's not—" he gasped. "It's not—I'm imagining things..."

"Are you sure?"

Guy started to nod, which turned to a frantic shake of the head, as though he could deny the evidence of his senses. This wasn't happening. This couldn't be happening. He was concussed, or hallucinating, or—

"I b-buried him," he choked out.

The creature chuckled again. Guy sensed movement behind him as it started to lean closer, caught a waft of its hot, fetid breath.

"And you thought that was enough?"

It was going to touch him. He couldn't let it touch him.

"*NO!*" Guy yelled, turning and raising the hammer high. There was the creature: dark, roughly shaped like a man, backlit by the glow from the square. Wings like black, ragged sails erupted from its back. But it was the face that stopped him from bringing the weapon down, the face that, like its voice, struck him with dreadful familiarity, like a dark reflection in a mirror. Not the features themselves, warped beyond humanity, but the *way* it was looking at him. Burning red eyes gleamed in victory. The gash of its mouth stretched in a slow smile.

"You buried his body," it said, *"but you'll never bury me."*

The hammer slipped from Guy's hand.

CHLOE HEADDON

Chloe Headdon grew up wanting to be either a writer or a knight, but since dressing up in armour and swinging a sword around isn't a viable life plan (apparently), she completed an English degree and a Masters in Medieval Studies before going on to work in marketing and heritage.

She writes fantasy and speculative fiction, with work published online in British Fantasy Society award-winning *Holdfast Magazine*, and has been a guest reader at BristolCon Fringe.

In her spare time, Chloe pursues her sword-wielding dreams as a student of Historical European Martial Arts (HEMA) and as a medieval re-enactor, both of which come in handy when writing fight scenes.

Follow her on Twitter @ChloeHeaddon.

All the best!

S-----

What Dwells In
The Mind

Scott Lewis

I am an old man now. Certainly older than I ever thought I would be, and possibly older than I deserve to be. I survived the mud of Flanders, the influenza epidemics of the early part of this century, and up until now I have survived the bombing of my home city by the Nazi scourge. But, I can say with utmost certainty that I shall not see another sunrise.

Thanks to a small article in today's *Post* and two chance sightings whilst going about my business earlier today, I know that I am doomed. Tomorrow, I shall be dead, and Hitler's Blitz shall not be solely responsible for my undoing.

The seeds of my destruction were sown thirty years ago.

For all this time I have kept my secret, and have dreaded to go anywhere near Temple Church, for fear of what lay beneath that accursed churchyard.

In the summer of 1910 I was in my second year as a psychology student at the newly-chartered University of Bristol. That erstwhile institution provided for those of my class and standing a reasonable education with the promise of further advancement into the profession. In years past I have returned several times to present lectures there; but for all my discourse on abnormal psychology and the treatment of those with mental illness, I never once touched upon that which caused me to question my own sanity.

I was joined in my studies by another local lad by the name of Arthur Drew, a sprightly young man, with an irrepressible smile and an untameable shock of red hair. He was, like me, of quite humble birth—the son of a publican and a washerwoman. He came from the countryside surrounding Bristol, out past Long Ashton and towards Backwell, and was attending the University on a scholarship.

When drunk he affected an attractive West Country lilt; sober, he attempted to disguise his upbringing by speaking as politely as possible, his accent tinged by a slight burr. He was my friend, and a great student of the works of Pinel and Kraeplin. He was also a man with distinct interests in refuting the theological approach to the diagnosis and treatment of diseases of the mind, and spent many hours researching cases of so-called 'demoniac possession', reading much of the stories of Elizabeth Knapp, Mademoiselle de Ranfaing, and the Loudun Possessions. It was this obsession that would bring about his downfall.

On the morning of August 17th, he came to my room with a report borrowed from the cellars of the public library. The report in question featured in a weathered copy of the late Bristol Gazette, dated 11 June 1778. A man from Yatton—a tailor by the name of George Lukins—had been seized by extreme fits and unusual behaviour. In his delusions he would utter mad, animal-like sounds; he would bark like a dog, argue violently with himself in different voices, and twitch unnervingly. By his own telling he had been experiencing these fits ever since a strange occurrence whilst performing in a mummer's play. Whilst on stage, he felt what he referred to as a 'divine slap' and was possessed by a fiendish spirit from that moment on.

In Lukins's case Arthur saw many of the symptoms of what Bleuler had characterised in 1908 as schizophrenia, or at least some particularly violent form of psychosis or epilepsy much like it. Arthur was largely agnostic—at times almost an atheist—in his approach to religion; it galled him that people would blame serious, treatable conditions on mere superstition. He was almost Hippocratic in his belief that such conditions were not, could not be, divine in origin, rather, they were an illness originating from within the brain itself. Thus began his quest to discover what had truly happened to George Lukins.

It was easy, with a short spell in the archives of the city's Central Library, to determine the common history of the Lukins affair. Those of a mind can find the full tale of the Reverend Easterbrook's account, and the exorcism that followed, in a copy of Priest's *The Wonder of Nature and Providence*. It makes for quite chilling reading. I paraphrase here for brevity, for Easterbrook's account is a detailed one; however, tell this story I must.

* * *

On the 7th of June, Lukins had been living in poor lodgings in Redcliffe Street, when he suffered a seizure of such violence and magnitude that he had to be restrained by the local Constabulary. Witnesses to the event later testified that he was shouting and screaming and knocking his head violently against the wall, lashing out at those who came near. As news of the incident spread, a woman who lived nearby took pity on Lukins.

The lady in question was a member of the congregation of Temple Church, a short walk away from Lukins's lodgings. She recounted Lukins's tale to her pastor, the Reverend Jacob Easterbrook, who took it upon himself to visit the afflicted man. After a short interview, he deemed George Lukins indeed a victim of demoniac possession, and sought the aid of other clergymen from around the region. From his fellow Anglican pastors he found no-one willing to support his calls for an exorcism; instead he found unlikely allies in the Methodist supporters of Dr John Wesley. On the morning of Friday 13th a total of sixteen men gathered in the vestry of Temple Church; George Lukins, the Reverend Easterbrook, six other men of the Methodist clergy, and several attendants to restrain and support Mr Lukins.

Throughout the ritual Lukins thrashed and spoke in numerous voices, including singing an ode to the Devil in what can only be described as a female voice. He held many discourses with himself, each time claiming to be Satan, or some vile agent thereof. Eventually, after over an hour, the body of George Lukins grew still and silent;

the only sound in the vestry the ragged breathing of the unconscious man. When he came to, Lukins was far more lucid. He claimed he was no longer possessed by that which had tormented him, collapsed to his knees in prayer, and thanked all those who had aided him. From there, he returned to Yatton to live the remainder of his days.

Easterbrook's account, printed originally in the newssheets of the period and later cited in the works of esoteric scholars like Priest, caught the public consciousness. The story of George Lukins did the rounds of Bristol's gossip shops and rumour mills for several years until, like so many other artefacts of popular lore, it fell into obscurity. Arthur hunted for further references as to the life of George Lukins, but none were forthcoming. Desperate to prove that there was a medical element to the Yatton Demoniac's suffering, Arthur threw himself into poring over endless records in the Central library. He made numerous trips to visit his parents, from whence he could stage interviews with descendants of those who claimed to know the man, but of his fate, Arthur found no sign.

His fortunes changed in December that year, when Arthur received by post a strange package. Within moments he had thrown on his coat and hurried to my lodging-house. After I opened the door to his furious knocking he pushed past me and slammed the parcel down on my desk. He could barely contain his excitement as he pulled something from the canvas wrapping; a battered, leather-bound journal, stained with age. A note accompanied it, written in a shaky hand.

Sir,

I have heard through correspondents at the Central Library of your interest in the tale of the Yatton Demoniac. My grandfather often spoke of the man; you see, he worked as caretaker of the church in question, and was one of those present on the day of the exorcism. I think he would wish you to have this; it is a volume of his journal from that year. In it there are hints of things that I think need to be comprehended; I feel that as a medical man and a man of science you may see fit to draw your own conclusions.

Yours,

Mrs. S. J. Ramley.

I had resigned myself to being Arthur's accomplice in his search, and so I sat on the bed whilst he took the seat next to my battered wooden desk. He began to read the tale committed to paper by Mrs. Ramley's late relative, growing more and more excited as he did so. Again, I paraphrase.

Three days after the supposed exorcism, doubtless while the Rev Easterbrook was writing his account of its success, there was heard a frenzied banging on the door of Temple Church. The three caretakers opened it, to find a wild, thrashing George Lukins. The man claimed that the Devil was back, and that he had come to wreak his revenge on those who had wronged him. He crashed into the nave, smashing his way through pews and scattering bibles here and there, making his way towards the altar. His eyes, according to the manuscript, had become sunken, dark pools; his skin tinged a waxen yellow. As he neared the altar one of the caretakers tried to stop him; Lukins seized the man by the throat and threw him clear across the room. This distraction allowed the author and his other companion to bash Lukins across the head with a candlestick, dashing him to the floor where he lay still.

The three men looked at each other aghast. The exorcism had clearly been ineffective; now they had to dispose of the unconscious form of George Lukins. One of the conspirators suggested the perfect hiding place—an ancient sepulchre in the churchyard led down to a crumbling, slightly-overgrown tomb, unopened for almost a century; the burial place of some long-dead Elizabethan notary named Haworth. Taking a heavy hammer the men loosened the stone slab covering the entrance and dragged the unfortunate Lukins down into the crypt, laying it atop the stone sarcophagus of the resident within. Using wood and stone from around the churchyard they filled in the passage leading down to the tomb, then replaced the heavy stone lid and mortared it firmly in place. The three men vowed never to speak of what had taken place, and indeed said nothing as Rev Easterbrook's account of the exorcism of George Lukins made its way into the public domain.

As Arthur finished reading me this account, he grew more and more excited.

"We've found it, Simon. Don't you see? We know now where to find George Lukins's final resting place." He smiled, almost dreamily. "All that remains is to perform an autopsy, and I can prove..."

"Arthur, that body—if it even exists, and this isn't some flight of fancy—would be over a century old."

"Quite so, but even an abnormality in the skull, a deformity of some kind, would be sufficient evidence to propose a hypothesis."

The realisation of his intent took a moment to dawn upon me as he gazed dreamily out of my garret window.

"Arthur, you don't mean—"

"Yes, Simon, I do. Tonight. I know the area around Temple Church well; there will be plenty of revellers in the pubs nearby which will mask any sound. The churchyard itself is high-walled; we shall have the utmost privacy. I will collect mattocks and shovels; you try to procure hammer and chisel, and ready a bucket for mortar. This is our chance to study the anatomy of a 'demoniac' first-hand; let us not waste it."

Two hours past midnight on the morning of the 15th December, Arthur and I crept into the blackened churchyard. The verger had long since locked the church and departed for the night, and only the sounds of late-night merry-making could be heard as we skulked through the graves. Weeds and foliage grew rampant over the Haworth tomb, and it took us a good fifteen minutes to clear enough aside that we could see the slab beneath. Several times we had to stop, disturbed by sounds from the surrounding underbrush; in our minds a badger's rustlings were transformed into the approach of the local constabulary, and the hoot of an owl was the clarion call of ghouls stalking us as prey. We took care to leave as much of the vegetation intact, in order to replace it when we were done.

We chiselled as stealthily as possible at the lid, and in an hour we had enough clearance that we could move it aside. Arthur dropped into the tomb whilst I stood watch. He began to dig through the obstructions below, clearing the rubble from the passage that descended into the vault itself. After another hour, he broke through to the chamber where the notable Haworth and his more recent tenant lay. He called up to me and I followed him into that musty chamber; I admit my nerves were so on edge I gripped the handle of my mattock tightly enough that my knuckles shone a stark white in the light of the small, shuttered lantern Arthur held up.

The dry air in that square, eight-by-eight chamber of hewn stone cleaved my tongue to the roof of my mouth. Carvings and paintings from Christian mythology adorned the walls and a raised sarcophagus held pride of place in the centre of the room—the last resting place of its Elizabethan incumbent, sealed within and laid to eternal rest. Sprawled across the lid, as if dumped on top of it, lay the body of another man. The corpse had been preserved quite well in the dry air; the lips peeled back to reveal a rictus smile, and the skin had withdrawn and tightened around the skeleton, dark and necrotic. It was clad in the garb of a hundred and fifty years previous, and we both knew we were looking at the long-lost form of George Lukins, the Yatton Demoniac.

"It's almost perfectly preserved." Arthur gasped as he

moved closer to the body.

"But how? The atmosphere in here is nowhere near cold and dry enough to preserve a body like this."

Around this time my recollection of events becomes hazy. Arthur stepped forward and set his tools out by the side of the sarcophagus, his intent fully to take measurements of the demoniac's skull and, if necessary, perform an autopsy on the miraculously-preserved corpse in front of us. The state of the body, he hoped, meant that enough of the brain would be intact that he could extract it and examine it for any abnormality beyond that imposed by death and decomposition. So engaged was he in his dictation of his method that he failed to notice strange, singular stirrings within the shell before him. I am not sure what came first; his scream or the sudden movement as the corpse reacted to his touch, eyelids snapping open to reveal deep, dark abyssal pools. It grabbed Arthur and pulled the youth close, pressing its paperish lips and grotesquely-protruding teeth against his mouth. I thought I saw something pass from the mouth of the decaying husk into my friend. A moment later, the corpse collapsed to the floor, bearing Arthur with it.

I ran to assist him, but by the time I crouched beside them, all that remained of George Lukins was a sack of bone and withered flesh. When I put my hand on Arthur's shoulder and offered to help him up, he began to laugh. It was a long, low laugh, not something I had ever heard my friend utter before. He turned to me, his eyes wild, and I swear I saw an inky blackness beginning to creep in from the edges of his eyeballs. He thrashed and gripped his head, screaming.

"Simon! It... it's inside me! Get it out! Get it out!" His body was wracked with a sob, and then I heard again that hideous, foul laugh. His head snapped up to face me, and inky black pits stared out at me from where Arthur Drew's eyes had peered just moments before. The laugh pealed out again, and he grabbed my throat and began to throttle me, trying to dash my head against the corner of the sarcophagus as he did so. I did not know whether it was Arthur's latent strength or some by-product of the foul spirit that had taken him, but the grip was like iron and I strained every sinew in my body to resist my fate.

One hand grasped at Arthur's wrist whilst the other, flailing, found the handle of my mattock. I swung with all my might, and the grip around my neck relaxed.

Arthur stood before me, swaying. The pick tip of my mattock had glanced off the side of his head, and the shock of the blow was enough to break the demoniac hold on my friend. The blackness had retreated from his eyes, and he looked at me before collapsing to his knees. He gasped like a fish out of water, his voice weak and hoarse.

"S... Simon... run... run while you can. You've freed me, but... it's coming back. I can't fight him anymore. Go, seal us in here. I will fight, and when I feel I am going to lose I'll open my wrists with my pocket knife. Close the tomb, Simon. Tell no-one of what took place here."

My flight from that tomb, and the scrambled replacement of the rubble, the slab, and finally the mortar, was done to the backdrop of the sounds of muted struggle from within. At the last I thought I heard a howl of fury, and then, as I slammed the lid of the tomb tight and sealed my friend within that cursed sepulchre, I heard a deep, resonant voice that will haunt me until my dying breath.

"I will come back for you, Simon Chauncey. This is not the end."

I hoped that my service in the Great War would free me of my burden, that one of the millions of pieces of lead and shrapnel that flew overhead would find its mark and end my suffering, but it never did. I continued Arthur's work on psychosis, and became one of the country's leading authorities on the subject. Little did my pupils, colleagues, and patients know that inside, I had to fight every day to maintain my grip on my own sanity. Arthur's disappearance was never explained to the authorities, and though I know the truth I could not divulge his whereabouts until now.

For today, the 25th of November, 1940, the *Post* has printed an image of the result of last night's bombing. Centre in the photograph is the shell of Temple Church, and the bomb-blasted churchyard. In the corner, amidst a tangle of bushes, lies the rubble and remains of the Haworth sepulchre. If one looks hard enough, one can see a hole descending into the depths. A hole remarkably free of rubble.

Twice today I have glanced over my shoulder to see a dirty, tousled mop of red hair in the crowd just behind me. I looked out of my window earlier to see the same figure lurking just down the road. I am grateful to have had time to commit this missive to paper. I seal it now, and I ask for the forgiveness of any entity that may be able to save my immortal soul. My service revolver is fully loaded; if, as I believe, the first five chambers cannot stop the thing from coming to exact its revenge upon me, then the sixth and final chamber I will turn upon myself. That... thing that wears the body of Arthur Drew, that once was George Lukins and untold others before him, shall not have me alive.

Scott Lewis

Scott Lewis trained as a journalist, and spent time with the Sunderland Echo, BBC Somerset and as a freelancer in China before switching his attention to PR and marketing. He took up fiction writing in late 2012, and in 2013 he won the Bristol Festival of Literature Short Story Competition. His work has appeared in several publications including *Airship Shape and Bristol Fashion, The Kraken Rises!, The First Line Literary Journal*, numerous anthologies and several short story compilations.

When not putting pen to paper Scott is an avid board and wargamer, roleplayer, and amateur photographer. He enjoys hiking, outdoor pursuits and gallavanting all over the country doing silly things.

He lives in Bristol with his partner and their Evil Feline Overlord, and can occasionally be found on Twitter @GntlmnRogue.

Abra-Cadaver

Maria Herring

"About time, Mivart," Emily whispers in my ear. "We were just about to start without you. Never make it to these meetings on time, do you?"

Nope. Never do. Always takes me ages to walk from my place to here. The chapel where we hold our Friends of Ashwood Vale meetings. It's the moon. Can't help looking at it when it's full like this. That bone-white disc. The way the craters resemble a mouth agape. You'd think after four-and-a-half billion years nothing we did down here could surprise it any more. But there it is; that constant expression of shock gazing down on a constantly changing world.

"Doesn't seem like that long since our last one, does it?"

Emily's still whispering in my ear.

"What?"

"Since our last meeting." She tuts. "Anyway, stop talking. Mary's there."

Sure enough, there's Mary gliding out of the chapel, a thunderous expression on her usually placid face. Well there would be—she never summons us unless shit's going down in the cemetery.

"Friends of Ashwood Vale!" she calls. The susurration of whispered conversation ceases. "Once more our beloved cemetery is under threat from property profiteers."

Emily tuts. "They just don't know when to stop, do they?"

I shake my head, but not in response to Emily's question; another threat means direct action. I'm not fond of direct action. I'm not an activist. Never was. Don't get me wrong—Ashwood Vale is a beautiful site and worth protecting. I just don't like being a part of that racket.

Why are you a Friend then, Mivart? is what you're thinking.

Perfectly reasonable question. Answer: didn't have a lot of choice.

"Presto Property Developers," continues Mary, "are due to start work tomorrow morning, exhuming graves—"

A collective groan moans out into the night.

"—exhuming graves and uprooting trees. We can't allow *this* to happen!"

Her words disperse us. We're no longer gathered around the chapel steps, we're motes floating around the graveyard, specks in the night. We have no form, but we do have conscious-ness and now we know what's caused Mary's wrath.

A monstrous regiment of machinery. Stationary bulldozers secure the perimeter but the vanguard have already massacred ancient trees at the cemetery's entrance. Limbs lay ripped from trunks, roots beseech the night air, leaves are scattered and left to wither. Excavators loom in the darkness, metal arms poised for battle. One, eager to be blooded, sank its steel maw into the soil before its comrades, and now broken bits of Emily are stuck between its earth-stained teeth. I feel her wail of despair crackle through me like electricity. She shares her pain. Her pain fills us with fear.

We're under attack.

"What about our Friends outside?" cries Emily, when we've manifested outside the chapel again. "How have they let it get this far?"

"Not for want of trying, Ms Crawford, I can assure you," says Mary. "They've been campaigning ever since Presto first bid for our cemetery, but to no avail. It seems £10 million was too enticing an offer for the city council to refuse."

"And what will Presto Property be developing our beloved cemetery into?" Emily, ever the journalist.

Now Mary's thunderous face becomes a superstorm. "They're calling it Enchanted Heights. A gated community for the super-rich."

Ah. I can see why that would piss Mary off. She kind of hates it when the few benefit at the cost of the many.

"This is our last chance, Friends!" she calls out. "Will you come together once again to stop this destruction?"

Cheers sway the boughs above us. Copper leaves drift down among us. I lower my lids in an attempt to block out what will come next, but it makes no difference. I can see right through them.

"I give you Mike Presto of Presto Property Developers,"

says Mary, her voice dangerously low. The crowd boos in a way only this crowd can—some of us have had hundreds of years of practice. "He calls himself Magic Mike. Apparently he *makes things happen*."

There he is now, being dragged up the steps at the front of the chapel. A suit so sharp he slices the air while he walks. Hair slick as an oil spill. I can imagine him in his daily life; nothing to say but jargon, his only facial expression a greasy smile, his two greatest passions: himself and his money. The kind of person who doesn't have the 'emotional bandwidth' to deal with anything heavier than superficiality. The kind of person who likes to 'touch base offline' with his mates instead of just meeting for drinks like normal people. The kind of person who demands 360° thinking from his synergised workforce while he's out playing golf all day.

What a dick.

I bet being abducted by spectres wasn't a tread on today's strategic staircase. A spreading stain darkens the front of his trousers and I start to feel a little bit sorry for him. We're all booing and hissing, but to him it'll just sound like the wind's picking up even though the air's as still as death. He can't see any of us—not even Harry and John, who are doing the dragging—but he can feel our presence. There's a lot of anger out here tonight and it's heart-stopping. You know that feeling when you start awake in the middle of the night from a dreadful nightmare? Imagine that sensation, stretched out for the rest of your life. That's how Magic Mike's feeling right now. I see it in his bulging eyes streaming tears, in his sweat-soaked shirt and piss-soaked trousers.

Also because he keeps shouting, "Whatthefuck? Whatthefuck? Whatthefuuuuuuck?!"

Don't fuck with the dead. Because they'll fuck you right back.

"Magic Mike," says Mary. He can't hear her, he's beyond that now. She's speaking for our benefit. "You are charged with the wilful destruction of protected land for profit. This land is protected by us. Die with the knowledge that it is, indeed, you who is making this happen."

We all fall silent. We do every time. For me, it's because I'm equal parts grossed out and horrified by what comes next. I don't know about the others, but—

Emily tuts. "I hate this bit, don't you, Mivart?" she says. "I always find it somewhat distasteful."

All right, so now I know Emily's grossed out by it too. I hope everyone else's silence means the same.

The thing about spectres is we're basically pure energy. Focus that energy enough and you can pretty much do anything you like. Mary's pretty adept at this by now. With a grave look of concentration, she reaches over to Magic Mike and slices her fingers across his abdomen, through the blue silk of his jacket, the white silk of his shirt, the flaccid skin of his belly. Viscera pours out, pooling at his feet. It's enough to silence even him. Probably because seeing your intestines erupt out of you isn't necessarily something you'd expect to see while standing alone on the steps of a chapel in the middle of a cemetery in the middle of the night. The agony will kick in soon enough though and the silence will be broken.

"Arrrrrrrrrrrgh! Fucking aaaarrrrrrrrrrggggghhhhh!"

There it is.

And that's enough for me. A twat this Magic Mike might be, but butchery makes me squeamish. I close my eyes but instantly realise that's useless—my lids are translucent. Instead I drop my head to the ground to stare at my feet, uncertain that anything there will block out the horror-film sound effects permeating the air, but desperate to give it a try. I stare at my shoes. Are they my old Velcro ones from school? I haven't seen those for ages. Although I'm a little bit disgruntled that my family didn't bury me in my posh lace-ups instead. Through my shoes I see my socks. At least they haven't got any holes in them. Well, they hadn't got any holes when I was buried. Fuck knows what they'll look like later when I get up. And through my socks I see my toes. Ten slightly chubby toes, for now at least, tap tapping on the freezing ground, as impatient as I am to get this ritual over and done with. I'm starting to count the grains of dust I can see through the soles of my feet when I realise the screaming has stopped and the last echoes are fading to silence.

He's finally dead. Harry and John let the mutilated corpse tumble to the ground—John gives it a bit of a kick because he always was a vicious bastard—then all us spectres commence the orgy in the gore. A gorgy, if you will. I don't like it, but I can't help it. I'm swept along with the crowd. I'm smoke from a chimney—I have to go the way the wind's blowing.

Mary, Harry and John come down and join us, and it's not that long before Magic Mike is nothing more than a greasy stain on the ground.

Mary looks around at us. "It is time," she intones.

Usually, Emily tuts at that, but this time she looks eager. Must be the effect of seeing her own desecrated body.

I still fucking hate this next bit.

Think of nothing. Your mindfulness 'in the moment' techniques won't work here, nor will your yoga zen consciousness decluttering. I mean, think of *nothing*. I doubt you'll be able to; if you did, you'd be terrified. It's like comprehending the vastness of the cosmos as a quantum particle, or waking up during the death of the universe. That's what it feels like every time Mary completes the ceremony and my spectral form, all mist and thought, reverts back to corporeal form. It feels like forever. Universes are born and die, and their cycle starts over again by the time I'm back in the ground.

But as terrifying as the extreme agoraphobia of nothingness is, it's nothing compared to the extreme claustrophobia of being back in my coffin.

The mould and mushroom of decomposition makes me gag. I can't remember how long I've been dead for— too much of my brain's been eaten by worms and with it a large portion of my memories—but I know it's long enough for the mahogany of my final resting place to crumble into the flaking flesh of my corpse. It itches. But that's not the worst sensation, by any stretch of my imagination.

I feel everything. I've got some pretty ghastly full-body pins and needles going on here: ants, having feasted on my innards, are busy tending to their nest—their scrabbling tickles until I remember what they're tickling; the thick sludge of mud-infused blood starts to gloop its way through veins and arteries that likely have leaks; in my nasal cavity sacs of baby spiders stir at my sudden inhalation; my eyeballs are aswirl with worms, which really fucks with my vision.

My coffin suffocates. I have to get out.

At least if I'm moving, I can pretend it's my reanimation I'm feeling, not all those bugs who've made my corpse their home/food source, which, now that that source is moving, are trying to flee.

I claw my way out. It's nowhere near as difficult as the first time, but I still lose a finger and a toe on the way up. I suck in great lungfuls of soil as my body's mechanical memory kicks in. I feel the cool, moist weight of it, plugging up gaps that used to flow with fresh air.

Fresh air finally greets my face, whistles through holes where teeth used to be, tousles the remaining strands of hair sticking obstinately to my scalp. Gripping onto the base of my tombstone, I haul myself out of my grave, my feet scrabbling for purchase on dead leaves crisped with ice. My corporeal form does *not* have ten chubby toes—funny how I never noticed how necessary they were for forward motion until now when most of them are gone. I push myself into a standing position and prepare to walk down the long hillside, but my arm is yanked back, like a cardigan sleeve snatched by a door handle on its way past. I look back. Not a cardigan—pretty sure I was buried in a jacket anyway—but a swathe of skin from my upper arm. I tug until I'm free and leave it hanging on the cracked headstone next to the other desiccated morsels.

Withered immortals flow past me in various states of decay, lurching, gliding, slipping, sliding. Forty-five acres of overgrown cemetery are transformed into a bewilderness of undead. Some are like me; half-skin, half-bone and writhing inside and out with the life that flourishes on death. Others are barely skeletons, their matter reverting to dust and ashes that vicars are so fond of talking about. Others still are nothing more than clouds of particles in vaguely humanoid shapes. Whoever gets wind of us lot first isn't going to have clean pants for very long.

Before following the crowd, I look up: the moon has set. Pink fingers of dawn stroke the sky in the east, birds stir in their nests and mice dive back down into their burrows. My spirit feels a connection with the nature around me, but my physical body aches with hunger. It's not the hunger you feel if you've skipped lunch because work's been pretty busy. This is a violent hunger. A teeth-gnashing, soul-wrenching hunger that promises never to be sated. It terrifies me, because I know I'm about to eat and eat and eat, causing horror and destruction, but I won't be able to stop myself until the blood-magic's worn off.

Someone at the front of the crowd has picked up the scent so the rest of us do too. My head creaks to the left, no longer under my control, and my legs lurch forwards.

Through my wormy vision I see the entrance to the cemetery, but it's no longer a wide swathe of welcoming pathways inviting humans in to walk around the wildlife; it's clogged with metal. Metal taken from the ground and moulded into massive machines belching smoke and fumes into sky; machines with teeth and claws that will scratch and gnaw away the earth that had once been their home. Mindless feasting on the life in the earth that gives life to the Earth, devouring until it's all gone. But this earth is still my home, and home to the 170,000 undead that are now awake, hungry, and angry at this invasion. This invasion perpetrated by Mike Presto's Property Development company.

We ambush the garrison.

Those who arrive first cannot be sensed by the humans working the machinery because they're little more than breaths of air and gusts of dust, and do little more than irritate the eyes and skin or cause explosive sneezes. There's some jocularity at that, those loud sneezes penetrating the serenity of a new dawn, and the laughter rattles around the cemetery like dice in a bone cup. None of them has seen Emily yet, twitching and jerking up there in the excavator, then yanking to pull herself out from the between its teeth. She wrenches most of herself free, then tumbles to the ground in an untidy heap, landing with a sound like a newly lit bonfire. When she finally finds her feet, the laughter soon becomes calls of confusion, then cries of alarm, then screams of terror be-cause the first of us in corporeal form has infiltrated the Presto pack.

I'm still lurching past the chapel when they strike,

and the shrieks of pain and rending of flesh and clatter of teeth on bone fuel my raging appetite and I speed up as best I can. But with one foot missing most of its bones and both missing most of their toes, it's playing merry hell with my balance.

I see one. He's running straight towards me. I get it— fear has addled his brain and instead of running back out of the cemetery gates to safety he's decided it's enough to get *away*. He doesn't see me. His head is still twisted towards the carnage now unfolding on his first day at work. But I see him very well. I push my arms out in front of me, hands grasping in anticipation. I notice that there's no skin left on the fingers any more, just some tired strands of dried flesh languishing on my palms.

He skewers himself on my bony fingers, and it's only at that point he turns his head to face me. Colour fades and his face slackens as he realises he hasn't escaped at all.

There's a part of my brain, what's left of it, that's still human—this part talking to you. I understand terror and I pity this poor man whose life is truncated in the most appalling manner. I died of cancer, eaten from within by a monster that terrified because I couldn't see it and I couldn't fight it. Powerless to avoid my own consumption. That was a scary time. But this guy? He sees me. He sees me dig into his body and ruin the organs that keep him alive. I'm the monster without. And he's just as powerless to stop his own consumption as I am to stop consuming. With the blood-magic fuelling my momentum, I'm nothing more than a mindless feasting machine.

Does he deserve it? Probably not. He just came here to do his job. He wasn't going to live in the gated community that would've displaced the dead. He'll leave behind family that'll mourn whatever's left of him, and I bet they'll bury him in nice shoes, too. I'll try and leave them his feet.

How to describe the warmth? I burrow my fingers further and further into his chest because his warmth revitalises me; blood like hot honey rushes over my crumbling forearms and I plunge my fingers into his heart, still beating for now, and I marvel at the movement of life. But only for a moment. The hunger envelops me utterly now. I yank his heart towards my mouth, ripping asunder his ribcage and drenching myself in his blood. A frenzy of feeding begins and unparalleled joy embraces me as my dead body is once more flooded with sensations.

As one, we all become aware that there are no living humans left in the cemetery. Myself and a few other corpses—I can never recognise anyone in corporeal form—are poking through a pile of bones devoid of flesh and marrow now. They're all that remain of the fleeing men, apart from tatters of bloody cloth and a splintered hard hat. Our awareness indicates that the blood-magic is finally wearing off, the threat's been neutralised and it's time for our postprandial nap.

It's a much steeper climb up the hill with such a full stomach.

* * *

"Honestly, Mivart," Emily whispers in my ear. "You could at least try to make it to these meetings on time."

I shrug the memory of my face at her, but it's really not my fault. It's the moon's. I've never seen it look quite so... different. The last time I was up, it was a big fat face staring down at me. Now that face is split in two, and those halves are separated by a column of sparkling lights. I'm pretty sure I see lights flashing on the surfaces of the half-moons, too. How long has it been?

"Friends of Ashwood Vale!" Mary calls. The susurration of whispered conversation ceases. "Once more our beloved cemetery is under threat from property profiteers."

Honestly! How many times do I have to tell you? Don't fuck with the dead. Because we'll fuck you right back.

MARIA HERRING

During the day Maria is a perfectly normal English Literature and Language teacher, but after 3.30pm she lets her SFF geek out. So far, that's got her two published novels (*Legacy of a Warrior Queen, The Book of Revelations*), a bunch of short stories, and a literary agent for her current grimdark sci-fi novel, *Locked World*. She wrote this book while living in Bristol, and acclaimed SFF novelist Liz Williams mentored her through the rewriting and editing process.

Now living in France, Maria is still a proud (and long-distance) member of the North Bristol Writers group. She has a fat tabby cat called Bilbo and is addicted to tea.

Find more information about Maria and her writing at www.mariaherring.com.

The Silent Scream

TANWEN COOPER

The dead had always screamed louder than the living to Lucy. It made it hell when she had to go into graveyards like this one.

When she'd been little she'd thought the austere walls around Victorian cemeteries kept in the screeching dead. Now she knew they kept people like her out.

Avoiding the streetlights, she slipped into the shadows near the faux-Roman gatehouse and skirted around the walls of Arnos Vale cemetery. The boundary muted the worst of the yells, but the chattering grew louder as she approached the loose fence boards and the voices seeped through the gaps.

Lucy paused to weave the barriers around her mind, then used the blade of her shovel to prise open the fence. Even with her precautions, the horde of voices assaulting her mind felt like jumping into ice water. Her breath refused to come and she struggled to stay standing while her mind acclimatised to the sound of a hundred thousand souls.

And her grandmother wondered why she preferred to use her talent pretending to be a fortune teller to messing about in graveyards.

The shock wore off and Lucy slipped through the fence, scanning the area to make sure she was alone. Strangely, she'd always found graveyards' living custodians caused her the most trouble—a creature of the aether couldn't exactly call the police on her. She'd still run the second she felt a Grim's presence, though. Those dogs might be spectral ones but the scars on her legs showed how real their teeth could be.

Casting about with her talent, Lucy knew she was alone. She stayed wary, though, as she moved through the trees that sprouted up through the cracks in the graves. Eyes forward she forced herself to see the world as it was, and not let the darkness twist the branches into horrors reaching out through the night.

Lord, she wished she could have done this during the day. The place had been filled with the living enjoying the autumn sunshine, the hum of their thoughts so contented Lucy hadn't wanted to drown them out, even if she had had the medication to do so.

But the dead? They had an eternity with nothing to do but shout a lifetime's regrets into the void, hoping someone would hear.

This was going to be a long night.

Lucy threaded her way through the undergrowth, seeking out landmarks she'd noted that morning. There was the crying angel lilting to one side. Now the obelisk towering over the graves of lesser men. Next should be the anchor weighing down a sailor's grave.

Searching the gloom for the marker, she spotted it tucked away behind a yew tree. She strode towards it, but her foot caught and she stumbled. A sharp stab of pain spiked through her knee as she landed on it hard. Lucy pushed herself back up, rubbing the soreness from her knee and cursing the root that had tripped her. This place was on the verge of being swallowed whole by nature, returning the dead back to the earth where they belonged. She'd have to watch her footing more. At least she hadn't torn her jeans.

"Give me my baby!"

The shriek tore through Lucy's distraction, flooding her with adrenaline. Every movement became an enemy. Waiting. Watching. They'd catch her, call the police, call the nurses to take away Loony Lucy. Their hands were already around her wrists, pressing down on her chest, she couldn't breathe, couldn't run, couldn't get away...

Lucy forced herself to focus on the smell of the earth, her rational mind wrenching the rest of her out of the past. She forced herself to breathe. The air tasted clean, not poisoned by the sweat of those who wanted to confine her. Lucy dug her fingers into the ground, helping her body remember where it was. That it was safe. The dead couldn't hurt her. This was just an anxiety attack because she'd had to ration her clozapine. The antipsychotic worked to calm the voices in her head just as well as if they had been imagined, but the withdrawal symptoms were still as keen. Few things would trigger an anxiety attack like the cry of a mother screaming for the baby she would never find.

Just a few more hours and she'd be able to get some more clozapine from Sparky without risking getting sectioned under the Mental Health Act for the privilege.

Lucy'd known her talent was real since she'd been eight and used it to cheat her way through a test on a book she'd never read. Not that the doctor had paid attention. The second Lucy mentioned she could hear voices, he'd decided she was crazy. Her efforts to convince him otherwise had ended up with a trip to the mental hospital. People didn't trust what they couldn't understand.

Lucy got to her feet, leaning on the shovel for support, and rewove the defences in her mind before continuing on. It wasn't far to the simple gravestone she was looking for. It still bore the roots of the ivy that had been cleared away from the whole area in an attempt to preserve the monuments. It was unfortunate that in doing so, the caretakers only prolonged the torment of the dead. Despite the damage, Lucy could make out the name and date.

Walter Cooper. 5 April 1780 - 17 June 1854.

Above the dead man's name was a badly hewn relief of a unicorn. Ironic, Lucy thought, that a creature renowned for its innocence should watch over a man who had made a fortune in slavery. But then it had been the patron animal of Bristol for hundreds of years and never raised a hoof to stop the trade of flesh that funded the port.

Lucy knelt down at the graveside, legs still unsteady. But if she didn't do this now, she'd end up in a worse state when her drug supply completely ran out. Slowly, she dropped her defences.

For a moment she couldn't breathe from the onslaught. Her instinct told her to flinch away but she forced her guard down, letting the thoughts of the dead flow through her until it felt like her skull was about to crack. She leant against the grave, hoping the physical support could help with the mental load.

"Walter?" she said. "Walter Cooper."

"A third dead in the hold. Is this my punishment for a third dead?"

"Why can't I feel the rain anymore?"

Lucy searched the voices to find the one she needed.

"I was a bad boy, papa always said."

"They'll never get it. Never."

"Mr Cooper!" she shouted at the voice, latching on to it, feeling its texture in her mind. "Mr Cooper is that you?"

"It will always be mine," he said again. As she focused on the voice, the others fell away like a radio tuning in.

"Walter Cooper? Of Cooper Enterprises?" she said.

Sometimes the older ones needed help remembering who they were. Time tended to fracture the psyche.

"Yes. That was my name. Walter. Why am I here?" he asked. *"It's so lonely."*

"Yes. You died. Unavoidable I'm afraid, happens to everyone."

Not everyone dies of pneumonia because they were too cheap to use their fortune to pay for firewood, she thought before catching herself. The last thing she needed was for Walter to catch the colour of her own thoughts.

"Dead? Then should I not be in heaven? Was I not a good man?"

No, you were not, thought Lucy. Not if half of what

she'd read was true. Even his obituary referred to him as a miser. But what had his penny-pinching ways earned him? A lonely grave with no-one to care for him but an ill-made unicorn.

"This isn't Hell," said Lucy. "Unfortunately, you got a full Victorian burial with all the trimmings, and now your soul is oh so snug in a stone box that will take the best part of a millennia to crack open and let you out."

The thought made Lucy's skin prickle. It might be the family tradition to spend eternity in a place like this, playing therapist to the dead, but to Lucy it sounded more like Hell than fire and brimstone ever would.

"I'm trapped here?"

The voice began to whimper.

"You would be," she said. "But today is your lucky day, because your friendly neighbourhood medium is here to help."

"You can save me..."

"Yup. I can dig you up, then drop you off somewhere you can return to the land from whence you came. Even brought my shovel, see." She tapped the blade on the stone.

The grave was brick-lined and far too solid for her to dig him out tonight, of course, but the show helped convince them. She'd find a way to keep her side of the bargain though. She always did.

"Please... it's so cold... so lonely..."

Lucy was beginning to feel the cold herself, seeping into her muscles and making them seize. When this was over, she was going to get herself a decent coat that didn't let the wind through. Hell, when this was over, she might just move somewhere warm. Somewhere where they cremated their dead, instead of throwing every nameless drug addict that wound up dead on the street into a mass grave.

"I can get you out, but in return, there's just one thing I need from you," she said. "Mr Cooper, in life you were a frugal man with a sensible distrust in the British banking system. A man who kept all his worldly wealth in gold rather than in the bank. Only, before you died, you buried that gold, didn't you Mr Cooper?"

"They took my slaves, but they'll never have my gold!" Rage built over a century flowed into his voice.

"And they didn't, Mr Cooper," she soothed. "You buried your treasure so well nobody could find it. People have been looking for decades."

People who had written very helpful books and websites about every known facet of the life of one Mr Walter Cooper. Lucy would have to thank them one day.

"They can't have it." His voice was harsh and possessive. *"It's mine."*

Lucy frowned. He'd been in the ground too long, with nothing to think about but his own avarice. As much as he may long for oblivion, Walter's greed was too deeply ingrained for him to pay the cost. She was going to have to take another tack.

"If it's yours, why isn't it with you?" She could feel the longing as he yearned to be reunited with his wealth, but it quickly turned black with jealousy.

"Can't trust them!" the voice hissed, joined by a hatred that wrapped its fingers around Lucy's heart and squeezed. *"The abolitionists took my slaves, now they'll*

take my gold. Never find it now. Never."

Lucy opened up her mind and focused on the smell of the earth around her as she pictured herself burying the gold in the grave beside him.

"But it should be with you," she said. "You and your fortune, together forever. Wouldn't you like that, Mr Cooper?"

There was a hiss of contentment and she knew he could see the false thoughts she conjured in her mind.

"I could bring it to you. All you have to do is tell me where the gold is."

His longing pulled on her own gut. She pictured herself digging in the ground. She imagined how her muscles would ache after hours of digging, the elation of finding the box, opening it up and cheering as she finally got her hands on the gold.

"You want to take it!"

Too late, she realised her mistake. Instead of reassuring him, she'd shown her true intent.

"No," said Lucy. "I don't want to take it. I want to bring it to you. The gold wants to be with you, its true master. It wants to come home."

"You can't have it."

Lucy recoiled from the pain skewering through her brain, almost breaking the connection, but she managed to hold on. Walter was never going to give her the money willingly. She'd have to go deeper. It was dangerous, but Sparky couldn't be fobbed off any longer and she needed her drugs. At least without them in her system her senses were sharp as she focused her entire consciousness on Walter Cooper.

"You buried the gold." She threw the words at him with the force of her will.

"The gold. The gold was all mine."

She leaned into his thoughts until all that made up the world was the glint of the gold in her hands. Walter's arthritis seeped into her own joints, seizing them up into claws.

"You put it in a box."

The feeling of wood grain ran over her fingertips as she caressed the casket, trusting it to carry her precious cargo.

"You took it away where no one would find it."

The cold air stung like daggers in her lungs. Dawn was kissing the horizon and her task was nearly done. Stretching out the stiffness from her spine, she leaned against the oak tree that would stand guardian over her beloved gold. Some young lovers had carved their initials into its trunk. Romance had never appealed to her, far too messy not to mention expensive, but their vandalism provided a distinctive marker to find the tree when she returned to claim her beloved. She looked out across the clearing to the turreted building some philanderer had raised in one of the most colossal wastes of money she'd ever seen.

"Blaise Castle," she shouted in triumph. "You buried it on the hill by Blaise Castle."

"What?" said Walter.

"Got you, you cheapskate bastard." She laughed bitterly, pounding the stone beneath her. "You could have been free of this hell of an afterlife, but no, you didn't want to make a deal. Have fun stuck here until judgement day."

Finally. She would be free. She could pay off her drug dealer, get enough clozapine to last her a year and run away forever.

Pain struck her in the ribs. For a moment, Sparky stood over her once again. She better pay her dues or it was a knife next time. But as quickly as the memory came it went, leaving only her panting in its wake.

"I can see you." Walter's tendrils snaked into her mind, picking her memories apart.

Back in the hospital, doctors told her to swallow medication that made her feel dead inside. She knew their secrets and it scared them. Their hands smelled of peach soap.

"You're a madwoman?"

In the schoolyard they chanted at her. Loony Lucy. Loony Lucy. Their thoughts were filled with fear without shape. Her grandmother admonished her that evening for not learning to keep her defences up against the slights in her classmates' minds.

"I'm not crazy," Lucy said out loud, trying to drag herself out from the sinkhole Walter was pulling her into.

Another time. A bedsit. Her grandmother stood in the kitchen, shaking her head at prescription bottles with other people's names on. "The talent is a gift to help those in need," grandmother said. Not a way to fund her drug habit. But Lucy won't risk the doctor's locking her up again. It was the last time she'd seen her grandmother alive.

"You are alone too," said the voice. The sympathy

angered her.

"I'm nothing like you," Lucy said grinding her hand against the stone to keep herself in the present. "I am alive. I am free. And soon I will have enough money to do whatever I damn well please. Have fun spending the rest of eternity knowing I've got your precious gold."

"What? No. Stop! Someone, help me. Stop her!"

The scream seemed to rend apart the universe. Lucy tried to sever the mental link, but it was too late. She blacked out.

One.

The first toll of the bell woke Lucy. How long had she been lying there?

Two.

Lucy tried to stand but the knee she'd fallen on earlier was seizing up and refusing to bend after being pressed against the cold ground for so long.

Three.

She managed to struggle to her feet, her head aching worse than any hangover. But soon all this would be over. No thanks to Walter bloody Cooper. She spat on the gravestone, her phlegm dripping down the body of the unicorn.

Four.

The bell chimes seemed to reverberate in her head, emphasising the pounding behind her eyes. At least the miser had done something helpful—Walter's silent scream seemed to have temporarily deafened her to the uncanny.

Five.

Her aching began to give way to elation. She'd won. With the memories she'd plucked from Walter's mind, Lucy was sure she could find his hiding spot.

Six.

Lucy's first instinct was to run over there now and claim her prize. But her watch said it was already 2:53am and she was exhausted.

Seven.

If she got a decent night's sleep then she could spend the daylight hours hunting for a tree with initials carved into it, then come back at night with a metal detector to find the chest.

Eight.

For once, she allowed herself a moment to appreciate the beauty of the night, taking advantage of her spirit-deafness to listen to the music of the wind and the steady chiming of the bell tower.

Nine.

Hang on. 2:53am. Why was a bell tower chiming at 2:53am?

Ten.

The pit of her stomach seemed to fill with lead. How many times had the bell tower rung? Ten times? Eight? Too many for the hour.

Eleven.

Midnight. The bell tower was tolling midnight. The time when even a fractured consciousness like Walter Cooper could pull something out of the aether. Something she wouldn't be able to hear coming.

Twelve.

Lucy ran. The ground seemed to shift underfoot, as if the earth rose up to impede her flight, but she had to flee. Was she even running away or just speeding towards them? Every flash of moonlight on marble became eyes glaring out at her from the darkness.

The trotting of hooves echoed across the graveyard.

A horse? But graveyard guardians were supposed to be dogs. They'd always been dogs. A dog she could fight off, but a tonne of horse? Think. She needed to get out of here.

Her eyes caught the glow of streetlights from the main road and Lucy pelted towards them, hoping she'd be able to vault the cemetery walls to freedom.

Ahead of her, the shadows moved.

The clanking of chains sounded through the dark. A long horn emerged from the gloom. Its length was stained black, dripping blood leaving dark puddles on the path. Heavy breath raised clouds of mist in the air as the muzzle of the beast emerged into view. Gore seeped from the base of the creature's horn, staining its once white face. Its eyes were rotten sockets writhing with maggots, the moonlight glistening off their white bodies. Iron chains wound up the thing's legs, ringing with each step the creature took.

Lucy stood frozen, transfixed by the Grim unicorn, protector of Walter Cooper.

It scraped its hoof against the ground as it readied to charge. Lucy bolted. Hooves thundered on cobblestones, and she knew the thing was right behind her. She could hear it getting closer, closer.

Pain ripped through her shoulder as the unicorn slashed its horn with enough force to knock her down. Hot blood poured down her back as she struggled to get back up. The beast reared over her, but she rolled away before it stamped down. Lucy searched frantically—there had to be something that could save her? She was back at Walter's grave. The shovel. She snatched it and spun around, smashing the blade into the side of the creature's head.

It shied back in pain. Lucy swung at the creature again, but this time it swatted the weapon away with its horn, pushing Lucy back into the bushes.

The beast made towards her, only to stumble sideways, snapping gravestones as it fell. Trying to right itself, the unicorn's hooves slipped on the rough terrain. Of course! It might be a monster but it was still a horse—it couldn't follow her across uneven ground. Lucy stepped backwards, pushing her way through the greenery tearing at her clothes. The monster had already galloped around to meet her, but she kept running towards the orange glow from beyond the cemetery walls.

No matter how fast she ran, the creature always kept pace. She reached the wall, but there it was, waiting for her at the end of the row. It pawed at the ground before lowering its head and charging.

Lucy leapt.

Her chest slammed into the top of the wall, her feet struggling to gain purchase on the sheer side. Agony screamed through her shoulder, the blood pouring from it made her hands slick, but her body knew the cost of failure. Lucy found enough strength to let her haul herself up just as the monster thudded into the wall, horn scraping along the stone.

Lucy lay there, panting from the exertion. Below her, the spectre reared up, stretching out with its horn, but it couldn't reach her.

Ecstasy ran through her. A laugh bubbled up, shaking her entire body as she revelled in her triumph.

"Guess you're not so great at guarding the dead after all!" she said, struggling to right herself. "I stole their secrets from right out under your stupid snout. Why don't you just go back to whatever Hell dimension it was you crawled out of? Twat."

Flipping an obscenity, she turned around to drop down the other side of the wall when her abused knee finally gave out beneath her. Lucy reached out to catch herself, but found nothing but empty air as she tipped over and fell back into the graveyard.

She heard, rather than felt, the crack of her skull against stone. When she came to, the breath of the grotesque unicorn blew against her cheek and Lucy knew she'd lost.

She waited for the killing blow but the moment never arrived. In the distance, she could hear the bell begin to toll again. One last blast of breath brushed her skin, and then the creature disappeared.

Lucy lay there, too exhausted to even feel the pain. Wait, she couldn't feel anything. She tried to stand, but her limbs wouldn't respond. She tried to wiggle her toes, but they wouldn't move. She tried to scream for help, but her vocal chords had seized.

"*It was my wedding night,*" came a young woman's cry. The temporary deafness from Walter Cooper's final shout was wearing off.

"*I don't want to stay here forever.*"

"*Let me die.*"

The yell of a thousand dead minds railing against the Universe that had wronged them beset her mind. Lucy tried to raise her barriers but she was too spent. For hours she could do nothing but listen to other people's agony, unable to even cry to relieve the torment. When she felt the familiar fuzz of a living mind, her soul wept in joy, even if her body couldn't.

A moment later, she heard the rhythmic footfalls of a jogger coming towards her. Finally. Someone who could help.

"*Bloody drug addicts. Can't they go find some other city to pollute?*"

For a moment, Lucy worried the man would just leave her there. She tried to scream for help, but her body was still frozen.

"You know you can't sleep here, right?" said the man, approaching her but still keeping his distance. "Can you even hear me woman. Or are you too..."

The man's voice caught as his entire mind wrapped around one thought.

"*Oh Christ. She's dead.*"

Dead. No. Lucy couldn't be dead. She was still thinking. Still feeling... except she couldn't feel anything, could she. Not the ground beneath her. Not the brush of the air. Not the warmth of the rising Sun. Nothing except the cold.

Oh God.

Through the rising panic Lucy heard the jogger ringing the emergency services. Perhaps there was still hope?

No. She was dead. She felt it in her core. The paramedics would send for the coroner, do an autopsy. Would it hurt? Lucy wondered. Would they find the traces of medication still left in her blood?

Then what? They'd track down her next-of-kin only to find there was none. Just another tragically mentally ill woman with no one left to care for her. No ill-made unicorns would mark the stones over the pauper's grave she'd be left in. Forever. With nothing but the mourning of the dead to keep her company.

"When will this perdition end?" a voice called across the graveyard.

In the silence of her own mind, Lucy began to scream.

TANWEN COOPER

Tanwen Cooper wrote her first story about a family of mice at the age of seven while sitting under her bed. She has been spinning tales on the page ever since. *Tales from the Graveyard* marks her fiction publication debut.

By day, she is an astrophysics expert and space journalist (yes, that is a real job) writing under the name Elizabeth Pearson. She currently works BBC *Sky at Night* Magazine and regularly appears on radio and television as a 'talking head' expert on all things space. She is currently working on her first non-fiction book about planetary exploration which will be published by The History Press in 2020.

She currently lives in Bristol, playing board games and counting the days until she can finally get a dog.

Blood Thicker Than Water

Piotr Świetlik

"**A**nd what the fuck do you know about migration?" It wasn't the first time he thought her obscenities stood in bright contrast to her delicate beauty and full, kissable lips. He caught himself staring again, cleared his throat and took a quick sip from the plastic bottle of cider. It was the third night in a row that they'd met by the river to share a drink. The first two, they mainly stayed silent and he wasn't expecting her to show up again, but she did and he was glad. The fact she wore no clothes was an added bonus.

"A thing or two. I've been places..." He didn't like to think back to those days, though. Too many skeletons in the closet. He giggled at the thought. His current address seemed just right to ponder such things.

"Right," she said, swinging her feet off the riverbank, her toes creating ripples on the surface. Enchanting. Mesmerising. He found himself drifting. "Hey! Stay with me, all right?"

"Mmm, what? Yeah, sure, sure." He cleared his throat again. He wasn't sure she was real but decided he should stay focused. In case she was. "So, you still haven't told me where you're from?" he offered her the bottle but she just shook her head absently.

"East. I used to live in Karachay. It's a lake, you know? Or at least it was until those bastards of yours came and poured death into it."

"Hey! They're not 'my' bastards. Whoever they are," he said, knowing she just meant humans in general.

"Yeah, anyway, after that it took me a while to find a place I could call my own. It ain't easy, you know? The real estate market in my niche is not exactly booming."

"Oh."

"Oh, indeed," she stretched out her arm and, full of surprise, he handed her the bottle. She took a long sip, a good half pint in one go, gave the cider back. "I..." she burped suddenly and giggled.

"Bless you."

A sideways look, followed by more giggling.

"I finally found this neat little lake called Rospuda. Clear water, plenty of fish, superstitious peasants nearby. All that a girl like me needs, really. And it was good for a while."

"So what happened?"

"The same as always. They cut the forest, polluted the water. Fish died and peasants moved to the cities or became 'farmers'. Can you imagine? Farmers, my arse!"

"I get the picture."

"Good. So, I had to move again. A friend recommended I moved to Avon, to the city. He's from London, you know? Big city, lots of canals and cemeteries, plenty of stupid people."

"Yeah, I visited." A flash of memory from a previous

life, previous reality.

"So anyway. He hooked me up with his friend and he helped me to settle in there," she pointed behind with a pale green thumb. "I had the whole neighbourhood to myself until you came."

"I'd like to think I'm a good neighbour," to prove his point he took a quick sip and passed the bottle to her. She didn't refuse. His hopes went up. Perhaps he'll finally get laid tonight. Her green skin and hair didn't bother him, he wasn't picky. Besides, he'd had none since he lost his home. No dating clubs for homeless widowers.

"You're all right, you know?" she slurred slightly. "For a human, that is."

"Well, on behalf of mankind, I thank you, my lady."

She gave an unpleasant smile showing rows of small sharp teeth. Suddenly all his game was gone, replaced by some primal dread.

"I'm no fucking lady," the teeth were gone, she was smiling again, stretching her green naked body in the moonlight. "I'm getting tired of it all."

"I can go if you want..." he said half hoping she would say 'yes'. Despite the hot July night, he felt a shiver run down his back.

"No, stay. You still haven't told me much about yourself."

He shrugged.

"What's there to tell? I'm broke, drunk, old and my current address contains the word 'cemetery'. Not much beyond that."

"Shame," she said quietly to the ripples.

She was quick like a nightmare. Her body twisted,

turned and he suddenly found himself on his back, pinned to the concrete by her small, unrelenting hands, staring into ancient terror. She looked just like in the old books his father kept, full of legends, unforgiving spirits and indifferent deities. His thoughts flitted to the rhythm of cheap cider pouring out of a knocked bottle. A pair of cold, milky white eyes observed him from a distance he'd hoped for just minutes ago. Flared nostrils shivered slightly, sniffing for something. And the teeth. God, the teeth, made him want to poke his eyes out, just to get rid of the image.

"You smell familiar," the slur was gone from her voice. "Where are you from? What's your lineage?"

"I... I... My family moved from Poland when I was little," he managed through trembling lips.

"A kinsmen. Shame. But a girl has to eat, you understand?"

Not knowing what else he could do, he nodded his head. He was expecting to feel the warmth of her body against his but she was cold like a tombstone. Her eyes narrowed.

"Real shame. I enjoyed talking to—" a loud splash interrupted her. She twisted her head to check the river and his face was covered by few strands of green hair. It felt cold and smelled of camomile and St John's Wort. "Saved by the bell, as the saying goes," she whispered into his ear and was gone.

A few moments later he heard thrashing in the water, not far downstream from where he lay, heart pounding, head empty of coherent thoughts. A scream, high pitched: male. A drunken cry for help, cut short by gurgling and sounds of struggle. Then nothing. Just his pulse thumping.

He sat up allowing his shaking hands to find the plastic bottle. There wasn't much left, but it was enough to stop the tears. He almost threw the empty bottle in the river then decided it would not be wise. It was time to get back home. Walking across the empty car park on River Road he thought he should, perhaps, move. Find somewhere else to live, to exist. He knew he wouldn't. She was the only one who still spoke to him, especially after he started sleeping in an old tomb which had marked his face with some kind of fungus. He tossed the empty bottle into the bin like the good citizen that he'd struggled to be his entire life. There was no traffic on Bath Road this time of the night so he took to the middle of the street. Some hundred yards ahead, the twin gatehouses of Arnos Vale Cemetery loomed in the street lamp's light. The wanderer was going home.

Piotr Świetlik

Piotr Świetlik was born and bred in the Silesian City of Chorzów, Poland. For over a decade now, he's been a citizen of the lovely town of Frome, where he is busy working on his first novel.

His stories appeared in *Airship Shape & Bristol Fashion* from Wizard's Tower Press, *Kraken Rises* from Angry Robot, on *365 Tomorrows* and most recently in *This Twisted Earth* anthology. He is half-responsible for the *Final Frontier* weekly radio show that runs on FromeFM, and the man behind psytrance project *Firefly*. He is also the creator of the *Sphere* role-play game and is currently working on an educational board game for kids.

One of his stories has been compared to Roger Zelazny's work, which set his ego loose on the world. He's still searching for it.

You can find out more about him at
www.piotrkswietlik.wordpress.com

Messenger

Alex Ballinger

After checking for messages, he sees the notification that had summoned him here—'Today is Aristere's birthday.'

Scuffing along gravel paths, amid the must of still-wet dying flowers, Leith rubs his hands as he checks he is walking in the right direction.

A glowing link on the screen offers to wish her happy birthday on his behalf. His eyes flicker from the name in bold on the phone to the cursive engraving lasered into the granite. His frustration grows with the inadequacy of his feeling as he faces her resting place.

The stone doesn't stand out—he expected something more *her*.

He types her name into his phone and her profile engulfs the screen, an avatar in one corner—a picture of three smiling faces, chosen by her.

He can't make out her face.

As Leith gently touches the picture, it fills the screen and his face jolts to a smile—Aristere's face glows with drunken delight, her arms around friends Leith knew by name but had never seen in person. He's jealous they shared that space caught on camera, chosen to sit in her final resting place online.

Swiping to the next picture, Leith sees her as she wanted to be seen, each photo chosen for the front page of her life. A picture of her in a sun-drenched garden, a beer in hand surrounded by friends, before they were together—Leith remembered her flirting with him as they poured drinks. Ari, in her graduation gown with her parents stood each side—they hadn't seen each other for a year or more, but he hadn't forgotten her. Ari at school—Leith had never told her he recognised his own shoulder in the corner of the frame.

With each picture she grows younger, until the images stop like paintings in pre-history.

Leith swipes back, as she ages in each frame until he reaches the end. No more updates. He longed for just one more virtual engraving, but she was gone too soon.

He remembers how his eyes burned from the tears as he stood in the crowd of her friends and family at her funeral. There he felt anonymous, like everything they had been was forgotten. He had thought he would never come back, but that was before he lost her feel as the mist of his grief lifted.

Returning to the main window of her profile Leith scrolls, longing for connection, looking for the things she said, the things she shared, the things shared with her.

Uncounted minutes scroll by, before he opens the 'about' section of her page, stifling a sob when he reads under the 'friends and family' heading. 'Friends'—they hadn't announced they were together. Regret punctures his growing mourning. Dragging his attention from the phone, Leith rubs the bridge of his nose with a finger and thumb, looks around the cemetery, then down at her grave for a moment, and with a scowl looks back to the screen, the backlight now faded.

'Send message'—the enticing words, not a question, not even a suggestion, a compulsion. 'Just a click' it screams. Send, but there would be no receive. Talking in an empty room.

With a slow move, jarred by guilt and capitulation like a gambler surrendering back into the washing disgrace of his vice, Leith taps the depthless screen.

Their final words appear, spectral white bubbles, disembodied and voiceless, no end to the conversation. Online it never really ends.

He reads:

> Yeah I've got work at 10 but I'll see you later this week

> You okay?

Leith had harboured some hope of a message fertile with prescience, something to give him an eerie shiver, ghostlike. But no.

He brushes a clawed hand through his hair. Hesitating, pausing, but persisting, he types.

> Hi Ari

The message pings into the void.

> **I don't know what the fuck I'm doing here but...**
>
> **I don't know how else to do this**
>
> **I just wish I'd made the most of**

"What the fuck are you doing, Leith?" he mutters out loud, his eyes never straying from the phone.

Then...

✔ SEEN AT 15:42

Leith retreats from the phone still clinging to his hand, his heart a bullet fired into the wall of his ribcage. Nothing happens. And then:

• • •

The pulsating ellipses of an imminent response. Leith feels numb as he considers the infinite immediate possibilities, from the likely to the...

A shrill ping sounds:

> I'm sorry, Ari is unable to take your call right now
>
> Please leave a message and I'll get back to you *beep*

Leith reminds himself to breathe.

"For fuck's sake." He reads the automated message she must have set up, probably smiling away to herself as she did. But then those dots appear again. Leith stares at the phone in disbelief and longing.

> Leith I'm kidding it's me.
> It's Ari, I'm here.

Horror, then denial. Was this supernatural, an algorithm gone rogue, or some new messenger feature to appease mourning users?

> Well, I say *here*

> I'm not entirely sure where here is,
> but you know what I mean

Leith's stare locks on the unnatural glow of the screen. He is afraid it feels so real, then slowly he tries to type, stops, erases the words, tries again but hits delete.

> Spit it out boy, the signal
> down here is terrible

> Kidding

Leith responds.

> This is a prank.

That's what you've gone with? That's your opening line?

Well I suppose you could be right

You never really know who you're talking to, do you?

Prove it's you.

Hmm...

How about the last thing I said to you?

That doesn't work, you can just scroll up and read it.

No you idiot, the last thing I *said* to you

Oh. I can't remember

I do – it's funny how clear my mind is now, a steady tide

I said 'you only like, never love.'

Why can't I remember your face?

Looking down, not out

Me?

Not just you

Will it get better?

Magic 8 ball says...

Outlook uncertain

Okay

We were always alienated

This is just the same

What next?

Might not be a next. Isn't that the point?

> Anyway, gotta go. God wants to use the phone

> Hahaha hah

> Ari

> Yeah Leith

> You know I loved you.

> KK ;)

The little green spot of life next to Ari's name fades into an X. The sun shines, and a gentle, cooling breeze flicks Leith's bare arms. He reaches to put the phone in his pocket, but pauses, holding it against his thigh. Lost in satisfied sadness, Leith doesn't notice the warmth of the sky above the cold stone of the graveyard.

His regret is swept away by relief as he remembers how it felt to have her just a fingertip away. Nearby, mourners kneel at the stones erected as reminders of life. His heartrate slows and doubt starts to seep through the cracks of his newfound solace. It couldn't really be her, could it? It must have been someone else who got into her account—a friend, or someone else...

Catching glimpses of names etched into crumbling stone, images flutter forth of wives and grandchildren and brothers that once mourned empty space, gathered around the markers and dressed in black—did they send something of themselves out beyond their bodies after they'd left it behind, even when their world had been so small?

In the distance he sees an elderly man in a wheelchair, sat beside a grave, motionless, his face a torrent, while Leith stands fearless, facing away from Ari's grave, an opposite image, clutching the phone. He pictures the lasting waves from these hundreds of thousands of pebbles dropped so lonely into the dark pond.

Alex Ballinger

Alex Ballinger is a journalist and writer from Lockleaze, Bristol who now lives anywhere work calls, currently Hampshire and London. He writes short stories and longer fiction often with a lick of philosophy spread across genres.

When away from his desk, Alex can be found (or lost) riding his bike in the depths of the countryside or else devouring newspapers and sportswriting.

His love of France resulted in his considering a French pseudonym for this anthology, but he thought better of it and writes under his real name.

Image Credits